Queen

KATEE ROBERT

*To everyone who was Team Damon, Team
Spike, and far too into Dimitri Belikov.*

Queen is a dark and incredibly spicy book that contains dubious consent, blood play, patricide, pregnancy, blood, gore, murder, explicit sex, vomiting (caused by pregnancy), discussions about abortion, abusive parent (father, historical, off-page), attempted sexual assault (alluded to, nongraphic), and attempted drugging.

Published by Sourcebooks Casablanca, an imprint of Sourcebooks
P.O. Box 4410, Naperville, Illinois 60567-4410
(630) 961-3900
sourcebooks.com

Also published as part of *Court of the Vampire Queen* in 2022 in the United
States of America by Sourcebooks Casablanca, an imprint of Sourcebooks.

Cataloging-in-Publication Data is on file with the Library of Congress.

Printed and bound in the United States of America.
POD

1

I NEVER GAVE MUCH THOUGHT TO PREGNANCY. NOT even when my father sent me to Malachi's home with the intention of sacrificing me, body and blood, to the trapped vampire. At the time, I'd planned on escaping or dying before he knocked me up.

Look at me now.

I slump back against the tub in the cheap motel bathroom. My head spins and sweat slicks my skin. My mouth tastes… Well, best not to think about that too hard or I'll start retching again. I drag myself up to the sink and brush my teeth for the tenth time today. An exercise in futility. I'll be puking again before too long.

As if being sick isn't bad enough, my thoughts feel as fuzzy as the inside of my mouth. I need to be planning, to come up with some idea to free my men, but I barely have the energy to move.

My father has Malachi, Wolf, and Rylan, and I should be coming up with a way to rescue them.

Instead, it's all I can do to navigate the crappy hotel room where I currently reside.

I stagger out of the bathroom to find Grace lounging on one of the two queen mattresses in the hotel room, flipping through channels with a bored expression on her face. I still don't know enough about this woman, for all that she's helped me. She's a white woman with long dark hair and an athletic build. She also seems to want to be anywhere but helping me. Yet she hasn't ditched me. Her pile of weapons is carefully arranged on the desk, and once again I'm left wondering about this one-woman army.

She glances at me and raises her brows. "You're a mess."

"I know." I drop onto the free bed and wait for my stomach to decide if it's going to rebel again. After a harrowing moment, it settles and I exhale in relief. "Did you have a chance to look over the plans of the compound I drew up?"

"Yeah." She sits up. "They're nicely detailed. You have a really good eye for security and what to look for."

Of course I do. I'd been planning on escaping the first chance I got. I had my father's patrols, security measures, and everything mapped down to the smallest detail, and I'd had to do it by memory because if I wrote something down and he found it... I shudder. "At least growing up in that hellhole was good for something. We can help the men." We *have* to help them.

"About that." Grace won't quite meet my eyes. "I'm going to be brutally honest with you—"

"When are you anything less than brutally honest?" We've

only been traveling together for two days, but Grace's bluntness is both a balm and an aggravation. She doesn't lie; she doesn't even bother to cushion harsh truths. I sit up. I'm about to get another of those harsh truths right now. "What's wrong?"

"It's a lost cause, Mina." She doesn't look happy about it. "If I had a trained team, we *might* be able to get in and get out, but the odds already aren't good because of what we're dealing with. By your own estimate, there are hundreds of vampires in that compound. Even if they were only turned and had no powers to speak of, those numbers just aren't surmountable. It doesn't matter that only a third or so of them are trained soldiers. Any vampire is a threat to the success of a rescue effort. Add in the fact that all your father has to do is speak and we lose, and it's impossible."

"No." I shake my head. This isn't right. None of this is *right*. Malachi and I were just talking about plans a few days ago. We should be safe in the mountain stronghold that is owned by Grace's family. We should be prepared to win.

Instead, I'm alone with a woman who obviously doesn't want to help but just as obviously feels obligated to try. And my men? They're currently enjoying the questionable hospitality that comes with being my father's captives. I shake my head again, harder this time. "I refuse to believe that."

"They'll kill us." She doesn't say it unkindly, and somehow that makes it worse. "If you're lucky, they'll kill you, too. If you're not, your father will lock you up somewhere until you birth that little monster and *then* he'll kill you."

I press my hand to my lower stomach where the little spark

of life pulses in time with my heart. "It's not a monster. It's barely a cluster of cells at this point."

Grace opens her mouth but hesitates. When I stare, she finally says, "It's making you weak. You can barely use your powers, and you're sleeping more than you're awake right now."

I drag my hand through my hair. She's right. I haven't been operating at anything resembling normal capacity since I found out I was pregnant a few days ago. I will admit to not knowing much about pregnancy, but it seems like the symptoms have come on far too quickly. I should have *weeks* before I start to see side effects.

Unless you've been pregnant longer than you or the men realized.

I clear my throat. "I know. It's not ideal, but—"

"There are options." She still won't meet my gaze. "You don't have to keep it."

I freeze. My brain knows what she's saying, but it still takes me a few moments to let the offer sink in. Terminate the pregnancy. I press my hand to my stomach. Hard not to be resentful of the little presence that isn't quite a presence. I thought pregnancy was my option to take my father's throne, but I can't even get in there, and I certainly don't have the energy to fight. If I show up and publicly declare myself his heir...

I want to believe it will stick.

I desperately need it to be true.

But there's a chance—and it's even a large chance at this point—that he'll do exactly what Grace says and lock me up until I have the baby and then kill me for all the trouble I've caused. More, my half siblings are hardly going to support my claim. As far as they're concerned, I'm a powerless dud, which means I'm not a legitimate contender for the head of clan.

If I had an army at my back, it wouldn't be a question. I could bust open the front gates, make my claim in front of the entire compound, and take over. No one could stop me. No one would *dare* stop me.

But with just me and Grace? And me being incapacitated more often than I'm not?

She's right to bring up this option, no matter how conflicted I am talking about it. "It's not just my decision," I finally say.

"Actually, it is." She shrugs when I look at her. "Hey, I'm not telling you what to do. I'm just presenting options. Ultimately, it doesn't really matter which way you land on the topic, because it's not going to change the end result. We have no way into the compound that doesn't get us both dead."

I wish she wasn't right. I press the heels of my hands to my eyes, trying to *think*. "There has to be a way." I have no allies. I wouldn't even know where to start looking for them, and it would take far too much time. Grace seems to be a lone wolf. Who the hell could we possibly call for... I drop my hands. "Azazel."

"*What?*"

The familiarity in Grace's tone nearly distracts me, but I'm too focused on what appears to be the only option we have. He asked for seven years of service to break the seraph bond I have with my men. We might not have agreed to those terms, but if he can do *that*, surely he can offer some kind of real help to get my men back. Even if it's the same price, seven years is *nothing* compared to potentially hundreds of years under my father's control.

I might not live that long, but Malachi, Rylan, and Wolf certainly will. It means there's no release waiting in the wings. Just endless suffering. I can't let that happen. I *won't*.

"*Mina!*"

I blink. "What?"

Grace is on her feet and looks like she can't decide whether to shake me or leave the room entirely. She rocks back on her heels. "Say that name again."

"Azazel." This time, I'm paying attention. I see the way she flinches and narrow my eyes. "How do you know that name? Do you know him?"

"No." A sharp shake of her head. "But I know *of* him. I know what he does." The way she speaks, it sounds like she's talking about more than just deals. Like there's an element of sinisterness to it I don't understand. Having met Azazel, I can't say he's anything less than terrifying, but he was rather frank about the terms. There were no hidden catches or trickery. It's more than I can say for how my father operates.

"He seemed fair," I say finally. "Or, if not fair, then honest." He spelled out the terms clearly. Maybe the contract itself would have been a problem, but we didn't get that far. The men drew the line at my paying seven years of service.

"Shows what you know." Grace paces back and forth in the small space at the end of the bed. She pulls her ponytail out and starts braiding her hair in short, agitated movements. "Are you aware of what he does? He rips women away from their families and most of the time they never return."

The way she talks, it sounds like she's speaking from personal experience. I frown. "Who do you know that's bargained with him? And seriously, he only bargains with women? That's kind of...outdated, isn't it?"

"Take it up with the demon." Grace drags her fingers through her long dark hair, disrupting her braid and restarting it. She's long since changed out of the camouflage hunting gear in favor of faded jeans and a plain white T-shirt. Somehow, it doesn't make her less intimidating...or less dangerous. She drops her arms and pins me with a look. "He took my mother."

"You mean your mother made a deal." I don't know why I'm arguing this. I don't owe Azazel anything. Wolf made it extremely clear how dangerous the demon is. If anything, I shouldn't be listening to Grace since she has just as much experience with demon deals as I do at this juncture. I wrap my arms around myself. "What were her terms?"

She turns away. "I don't know. The last time I saw her was the night he came to collect. I know she made a deal, but I've never been able to get more information. I..." She exhales slowly. "I don't know how to summon him. Do you?"

Do I?

I know what Wolf did. It seemed simple enough, at least in theory. His bloodline vampire power is the ability to manipulate blood itself. Thanks to my seraph half, I've somehow managed to acquire that ability, along with Rylan's shape-shifting and Malachi's fire. It *would* be enough...except I got these powers less than a week ago and I've had exactly one training session with Malachi to learn how to control them. Since then, I've barely had the energy to keep up with Grace, let alone try again.

I close my eyes and try to walk back through what Wolf did to summon Azazel. A blood circle that became a blood ward of sorts. I think. He fucked Malachi in it, but I don't know if that's part of the ward or just because Wolf is, well, *Wolf*.

As far as I can tell, after creating the ward, he did nothing at all. Azazel showed up quickly after Malachi and Rylan left, but Wolf didn't even say his name before the shadows went weird and the demon appeared. It has to be the circle. Which is a problem because I don't know the first thing about creating a blood ward. "Do you know how to create a blood ward?"

"Mina, I'm *human*."

Right. Of course. I shake my head slowly. "Then no. I don't think I can summon him." Then again, maybe I'm overcomplicating things? I lift my voice. "Azazel? Can you hear me?"

"Holy fuck." Grace flings herself back against the wall, her dark eyes wide as she searches the room. The seconds tick into a full minute, and we both breathe a sigh of something akin to relief when nothing and no one materializes. Grace glares. "I can*not* believe you just did that."

I can't believe I just did that, either. I shrug, trying to pretend I'm not as shaken as I am. "It was worth a shot."

"It was worth a shot," she repeats, shaking her head. "You are out of your damn mind, Mina." Grace scoops up her backpack from the floor and a small gun from the desk to tuck into her waistband. She pauses with her hand on the door. "Get some sleep. I'm going to see about taking a look at this compound myself. I think it's a long shot, but maybe there's something you missed or something that's changed since you were there that can provide us a way in."

It's not safe for her to go scouting on her own. My father is sure to have sentries farther afield than just the compound walls, and Grace might be human and therefore not seen as a threat, but she's a beautiful human. I wouldn't put it past them to try to snatch her off the street to either be turned or tossed into my father's pool of humans who serve as mistresses and blood banks. "Grace—"

She's gone before I can get my warning out.

I mean to follow. I truly do. But one minute I'm trying to get the energy to stand and move to the door, and the next a wave of dizziness hits me hard enough that I have to throw out a hand to brace myself on the bed so I don't topple. "What the fuck?"

Is this an attack?

I try to push my magic out, to sense, but it's like I'm wrapped in a thick cotton straitjacket. I can't feel anything at all. With a curse, I turn inward. A quick body scan leaves me even dizzier. *Oh no. This is so bad.* I let my hand drop, feeling ill in a way that has nothing to do with morning sickness. I'm not being attacked, at least not from the outside.

It's the baby.

It's draining my magic.

2

I DON'T MEAN TO FALL ASLEEP, BUT LIKE SO MUCH ELSE with this damn pregnancy, it's as if I don't have a choice in the matter. One moment I'm cursing my circumstances and the next I open my eyes to a strange room. It's not the hotel; it's nowhere near as concrete as that. The whole space feels strangely misty and uncertain, and yet as I sit up and look around, it also doesn't feel like a dream. Normally, when I dream, I don't realize it *is* a dream until I wake.

I feel awake now.

I push to my feet, waiting for a wave of nausea, but my body feels strangely muted. I inhale slowly and exhale just as slowly. For the first time in a week, I actually feel like myself. Nothing hurts. I'm not exhausted. It's enough to make me want to cry. I didn't realize how bad things had gotten until I was allowed this reprieve. I swallow thickly. "What am I going to do?"

No use focusing on the problem the pregnancy represents now, though. I have to figure out what's going on. Is this another trap? My father's powers lie in compulsion and glamour; I've never heard him talk about dreams before. This *isn't* a bloodline vampire power at all as far as I can remember. There are only seven of them, each following one family. My father's glamour. Malachi's fire. Rylan's shape-shifting. Wolf's blood. And then air, earth, and water. None of those should be able to influence dreams.

So what is this?

My chest gives a familiar thrum and I don't think. I simply follow it. It's the bond inside me, recognizing—I'm afraid to hope it's recognizing what I *think* it's recognizing. Distance and time have no meaning here. One step seems to launch me forward miles. Or maybe the mist is what causes everything to feel strange. I'm not sure.

In the distance, the mist rolls away and the familiar form of a man stands there. I recognize his pale skin, short white mohawk, and lean frame. The bond inside me thrums happily and nearly jerks me off my feet. "Wolf!"

He turns slowly, recognition brightening his light blue eyes. "Mina."

One step brings me to him. I reach out a trembling hand and press it to his chest. Real? Not real? I can't be sure. He looks even paler than normal, deep circles carved into the space below his eyes. "How are you doing this? How did you bring me here?"

"It's not me, love." He looks around, a frown pulling his dark brows together. "This doesn't feel like vampire magic. Means it's most likely you."

Me or someone else planted us both here. I look around, but there's still nothing but mist. I can't sense danger, but I can't sense anything at all. I didn't feel Wolf before I saw him, and even now, with my palm against his sternum, it's like neither of us are really here. "The bond?"

"That would be my best bet."

That's comforting, though I would feel better if someone had a full explanation. "Is this a dream?"

"It must be. I'm not hungry."

A pang goes through me. It's already started. Of course it has. My father wouldn't hesitate to put them into painful and agonizing situations to ensure he gets what he wants. I swallow hard. "It wasn't supposed to be like this."

"It never is when things go wrong." He shrugs, but his eyes go sharp. "You're close. The bond hasn't bitten us once."

"I'm trying. I knew where he was taking you, so I made sure to follow as closely as I dared." The bond is another problem to the huge stack of them. I found out relatively recently I'm half seraph by accidentally bonding with Wolf, Malachi, and Rylan when my powers unleashed. One of the lovely little side effects of that bond—in addition to these new powers I can't control—is that there's a limit on the distance we can travel from each other before we experience pain. It's worse for the men than it is for me. Distance isn't the only issue, either. Even if I stay within range, eventually the bond will force us closer. There's a physical component that I recently had to navigate with Rylan, and I don't relish the idea of having to do it with all three of them.

I hate it, but so far the only option we've found to eliminate the seraph bond is...

Azazel.

I straighten. "Wolf, I need to know how to summon Azazel."

"No, love. Straights are dire, but not so dire as that." He runs a hand over his short mohawk. "He demands payment up front, and I don't know what will happen to the bond and us if you jaunt off to the demon realm. Even if time passes differently there than it does here, that's quite a bit out of the established distance limits."

He's right. I know he's right.

But so is Grace.

I lift my chin. "I promise I won't bargain away my time like that. I'll think of something else."

"He's a one-trick pony is Azazel. It's seven years' payment. That's the only currency he works in." Wolf shakes his head. "It's not worth the risk."

I grab the front of Wolf's shirt and shake him. Or try to. It's like shaking a brick wall. Frustration blooms, hot and sick, in my stomach. "I have exactly two people to breach the compound. We can't win. Even with the pregnancy, we can't win."

"Even with the *what?*"

The feeling in my stomach gets worse. A pulse that becomes a thrum. I press my hand there and flinch. It's hot. Literally hot to the touch. "What the fuck?" Another pulse, hotter this time. It *hurts.* "What the *fuck?*"

"Mina, love, did you just say you're pregnant?"

I open my mouth to answer, but the mist around us swirls. No, *swirls* is too tame a word. It feels like what I imagine being in the middle of a hurricane is like. Phantom wind pulls at my hair and clothing, so strong it forces me back a step from Wolf. "Tell me how to summon him!"

He shakes his head again. "It's not worth the risk."

The fact that this comes from *Wolf*, who is arguably the most unhinged of my men, should be enough to stop me. To convince me to find another path. Instead, it only infuriates me. I agreed with them on passing on Azazel's last offer. It was the right call, but that was back when we had options.

I'm out of options and out of ideas.

"*Tell me.*" Power thrums through my voice, demanding answers, demanding obedience.

"Damn it, Mina." He hits his knees, and guilt tries to prick me, but I don't have time to feel guilty. He speaks in rough tones. "Circle of blood, charge it with your magic, focus your intent on him and him alone. He'll come."

"I'm sorry."

He shudders, slumping down to his hands and knees. "It's not worth the risk," he repeats. "He'll ask for more than you can safely pay."

It's worth the risk to me. I'd do worse than summon a demon if it means getting my men out of my father's clutches and to safety. "I can handle myself."

"You're making a mistake, love." The mist rises up and swallows him whole. I take a step in his direction, but there's nothing there. It's as if Wolf never existed. If we all survive this, then I'll deal with the consequences of using our bond to force his compliance. Maybe it makes me a monster, maybe he'll never forgive me, but at least he'll be alive.

But only if I succeed.

My body clenches in agony, jarring me from my thoughts. I double over, holding my stomach, and scream.

"Mina!"

I jerk away to find Grace with a freaked-out expression on her face and her fingers digging into my shoulders. She doesn't immediately let me go, though. She pauses, gaze searching my face. "Are you awake?"

"My eyes are open!"

"Yeah, they were before, too." She shudders and releases me, backing up quickly. Like she's scared of me. She glances at the door but then seems to change her mind about fleeing my presence. Instead, she walks stiffly to the other bed and sinks onto the edge. "What the fuck was that, Mina?"

I start to sit up, but my body feels like I've run miles and then climbed a mountain. "Ouch." I press my hand to my forehead, wincing when I realize I'm sweaty. *Really* sweaty. My stomach hurts a bit, but nowhere near like it did in the dream.

I sit up so fast the room takes a sickening spin around me. "I dreamed of Wolf."

"Honey, I don't know what you were doing, but that wasn't normal dreaming." Grace shudders again. "Your eyes were open and you had this aura… It was like some demon possession shit."

"Do demons possess people?" Wolf had said Azazel was a one-trick pony, but that didn't mean there weren't other types of demons out there. As I'm discovering, the universe is vast and has more than one realm. Even in this one, there are more supernatural creatures than vampires. I'm a prime example of that, for all that the seraphim are supposed to be extinct.

"No." She shakes her head. "They can do a lot of fucked-up shit, but possession was invented by the church."

That's right. She'd know, wouldn't she? I'm sure being from a family with a legacy of hunting monsters is handy when it comes to information about said monsters. They must keep records. "How do you know that but not how to summon Azazel? It seems like it should be right up your alley."

"My mother destroyed the records before she made her bargain."

So much emotion in such a short sentence. There are layers of history there, and I should care, but I can barely think past the current mess. When push comes to shove, I barely know Grace. I shiver, the air-conditioning icing across my sweaty skin. Whatever happened to me, it's over. For now. I think back through what Wolf did and didn't say. He'd told the truth when it came to summoning the demon, but his simplified version left a lot to be desired. No doubt that was on purpose since I'd had to compel the information from him in the first place.

Guilt pricks, but I shove it aside. I had no choice. He wasn't going to tell me, and I need this information to have an icicle's chance in hell of saving them. I'll work on earning his forgiveness after I'm sure he'll be alive and free to give it.

I press my fingers to my temples. Wolf said to charge the circle, which confirms my suspicions on why he was the one to summon Azazel. The blood ward *was* vital to the process, which is a problem because I don't know how to charge my blood. I only know how to bleed.

Life has never been easy for me before. No reason for it to break the trend and start being easy now. "Wolf said I need to make a circle, charge it, and then focus to summon Azazel."

"That's it." Grace sounds suspicious, not that I blame her. It sounds too good to be true. Too simple to work.

"Sounds easy. Is a lot more complicated in practice." I shake my head slowly. "Wolf is a bloodline vampire whose specialty *is* blood. He can do things that no one else outside his family can." No one except me, at least in theory. I swallow hard. "It's a power we share."

"You do." Again, the disbelief.

I still haven't told her about my seraph half or my bond with the men. Grace might have some strange allegiance to Rylan—or owe him a favor, as she says—but I don't know how far that, well, grace extends. She's a monster hunter from a family of monster hunters, and everything I've discovered about seraphim to date paints them as monsters even among otherworldly creatures that prey on humanity.

There's a reason they were hunted to apparent extinction by the vampires.

The amount of harm the seraphim did...

I can't guarantee Grace won't decide that I'm too much of a threat, even if I don't know how to use my fledgling powers properly, or even that the little cluster of cells inside me that is a combination of both seraph and vampire will be too monstrous to allow into the world.

I'm not sure she's wrong there, either.

I'm not sure of anything anymore.

"I can't control it," I finally admit. In fact, none of the blood-line powers have manifested since I fled the mountain home where my father had finally caught up with us and taken the men captive. I haven't thought too hard about that, but it has to be because I'm so exhausted all the time. "I'm not even sure how to begin to make it work."

"Well, shit." She slumps onto the bed. "Guess we're back to square one."

A hopeless situation.

I give her a long look. "Why help me? You got me out of there, which is repayment enough for whatever debt your family owes Rylan."

"Undoubtedly." She shrugs. "Honestly, I was going to pay your hotel for a week and then leave today, but now that I know you can summon Azazel—or at least one of those vampires can—you're stuck with me. I need access to that demon."

I don't tell her that her chances of finding her mother alive are low. Maybe they aren't. This world is strange and vast and odder things have happened. It's not my place to crush this woman's hope when I'm engaging in my own long shot.

I need my men back, I need to kill my father, and I need to announce this damned pregnancy publicly where no one can refute it to ensure my half siblings don't hunt me until the end of days just like my father planned to. I need to essentially crown myself queen the same way my father acts the part of a king. None of my siblings are as formidable as he is, but that doesn't mean they're not dangerous.

The only path to peace is through power, and it means taking my father's place as head of the compound...and head of the bloodline.

Ironic, that.

I hold three sets of bloodline powers inside me, but none of them were passed to me by my father.

3

I TRY TO EAT, KNOWING I NEED THE CALORIES FOR THE
bloodletting that comes next, but I last all of twenty minutes
before I'm in the bathroom, losing my lunch. Hopelessness wells
up inside me, deep and dark and all too willing to suck me under.

I've been in bad spots before. I was *born* into a bad spot, a
powerless dhampir in the compound my father rules. Normally,
dhampir children—those who are half human and half vampire—
inherit powers from their vampire parent, at least if said vampire
parent is a bloodline vampire. Not me, though. Up until I met
Malachi, Rylan, and Wolf, I thought I was defective.

Turns out my mother wasn't all that human to begin with.

I brush my teeth, staring at my reflection in the dingy mirror.
I look like shit. Dark circles stain the skin beneath my bloodshot
eyes and my dark hair has gone greasy and lank. I've lost weight,

too, weight I can't afford to lose. I was hardly at peak health when all this started, though the blood the vampires shared with me seemed to do just as much as...

I stop brushing.

Surely that's not the answer. It would be far too ridiculous a solution. If I managed to drink blood, surely I'll throw it up just like I'm throwing up solid food. I'm not some heroine in a vampire novel. I'm not going from eating normal food and using blood for magic, pleasure, and healing to being on a blood-only diet. It's not going to happen.

I duck out of the bathroom to find Grace gone again. I think she feels trapped in the hotel room. I don't blame her; I'm practically climbing the walls at this point. Or I would be if I had any energy at all.

This is a mess. Worse than a mess. It's a fucking disaster.

I study the bed for a long moment. I still haven't entirely dealt with the fact that apparently I met Wolf in my dreams. I don't know what caused it or what shoved him out of that space, but if I can reclaim it...

I miss them. I miss them so fucking much I ache with it. I wish I could blame the bond for the heightened feeling, but I suspect it's simply that I've gone and fallen for this vampire trio. I desperately want Malachi to wrap me up in his big arms and say it will all be okay. For Rylan to make some snarling, snarky comment about the situation. For Wolf's wild laughter and chaos.

If I can find them in my dreams...

I run my hand over the scratchy bedspread. I'm tired.

Desperately tired. I should still be using this time to practice the magic as best I can.

Instead, I take a slow, careful breath and lie down on the bed on my back. It's too easy to close my eyes. I've been sick and beaten to the point where I'm not sure I'll survive, and I've never felt tired like this. It would scare me if I had the energy to feel anything but exhaustion.

Maybe it's the baby, but maybe that's not it at all. Maybe it's the seraph bond responding to too many days and too much distance between me and my men. If they're suffering similarly...

Sleep sucks me under before I can finish the thought.

I open my eyes with a start. Disappointment sours my stomach—or maybe that's just the baby—when I see the hotel room exactly as I left it. The only difference is the light gone from the windows, replaced by the faded rays of the streetlamp outside.

Grace still isn't back yet, and if she was anyone else, I might be worried, but she can take care of herself. I saw how many weapons she packed away before she left. The woman is a walking armory, and she knows how to use them. She'll be fine.

I sit up and rub my hands over my face. Maybe the dream with Wolf was a fluke. Maybe there are a dozen conditions that need to be met before I can meet like that with any of the vampires. I just don't know enough. I'm in the dark and attempting to feel my way. I don't even have Malachi's support at my back while I'm doing it.

"What the fuck am I even thinking?" I stagger to my feet

and cross to the desk of Grace's weapons. There are half a dozen knives in varying shapes and sizes, and I choose a small one that fits easily in my palm. "I am not helpless."

I'm also speaking to an empty room, which might make me certifiable, but it's better than letting the silence tick out. There are too many things that can go wrong with what I'm about to do. If I think too hard, I'll talk myself right out of it. So I don't. I act instead.

I slice a thin line on my forearm and hold it out away from my body. It hurts, but compared to how everything hurts these days, it's barely noticeable. I turn in a slow circle, leaving droplets of blood behind me, until I'm once again facing the way I started.

My own blood smells savory, which is disconcerting in the extreme, and it only gets worse when I close my eyes and focus internally the way Malachi taught me. I can *almost* sense the magic there, lying in wait. It feels different than it did the last time I tried this, but I don't know enough to guess why.

"Come on, you fucker." I reach for the power with metaphorical—metaphysical?—hands, but it slips through my palms like water. I grab for it again, with the same result. Again and again and again. Nothing. Fucking *nothing*.

I open my eyes as I sink to my knees. My head spins sickeningly, or maybe it's the room spinning. I don't know what's real anymore. Certainly not this nebulous power inside me. I can't even access it without the men present. How pathetic. "Damn it!" I lift my voice, too loud, but I'm past caring. "Azazel! Azazel! *Azazel!*"

"You can't yell my name three times and expect me to arrive."

I jolt, losing my balance and landing on my ass in the middle of the sad little blood circle I created. One completely devoid of power. And yet here Azazel is. I lean back and narrow my eyes, trying to pick him out of the shadows in the corner of the room. I should be terrified. There's nothing protecting me from him, and the menace he seems to carry about him like a cloak is in full evidence right now.

He looks much the same as last time, a man with light brown skin, dark hair, and soulless dark eyes. Though no one with a brain in their head would look at him and think he's something as mundane as a *man*. He's a predator in a way even vampires can never aspire to be.

The shadows lick at his legs as he steps around the bed and stares down at me. "You've called. I've answered. Have you reconsidered the breaking of your bond?" He glances about the room. "Where's Wolf and the others? Did you finally acquire some sense and flee them?"

"What's with all the questions?" My voice comes out slightly slurred and I have to lean back against the other bed when the room shifts again. Damn it, what is *wrong* with me? I blink down at the red stain spreading across my jeans. For a horrifying moment, I think it's the baby...but no, it's nothing as traumatic as that.

I cut my arm too deep.

Or, rather, I haven't had vampire blood in days. A cut that would have healed already a week ago is now leaking blood steadily down to my thigh where I rest it. A lot of blood. "Damn."

"You little fool." He growls under his breath in a language

I'm certain isn't known in this realm and crouches down in front of me. He's no less terrifying up close. Once again, I get the impression that he's somehow bigger than he appears, that horns paint shadows across the motel room behind him. A blink and it's gone, but I can't quite convince myself I've imagined it.

He grabs my arm, moving too quickly for me to jerk away. "This will hurt."

"Wait—" Pain lances my forearm, so sharp and sudden, it draws a scream from my lips. Or it tries to. He covers my mouth with his other hand. Everything gets a little faded, but how in the gods' names does his hand wrap around the entire bottom half of my face?

Something is *not right* with this demon.

"There." Even his voice has changed, deepening with something akin to irritation. "Now you won't bleed out before you can accept my bargain."

I stare blankly down at the scar now carved into my arm. The cut was a straight line. This thing is...not. It's also red and black, twisted, and angry looking like a tree that attempted to uproot itself. "What did you do to me?"

"You can thank me later." He snaps his fingers in front of my face. "The bargain."

"I..." I lick my lips, trying to focus. "I didn't call you here to accept your bargain."

Again that hissing language that hurts my ears. He shoves to his feet. "Tell Wolf to consider the healing a token of our friendship. I have places to be."

"Wait!"

He pauses, but impatience paints every line of his body. "You're wasting my time."

"No." I can't stand. I'll pass out. I'm sure of it. Instead, I try to straighten a bit where I sit. "I want a new bargain."

He exhales slowly and turns back to face me. "I'm listening."

"My father took Wolf and Malachi and Rylan. I want them back."

Azazel considers me for a long moment, then his gaze goes distant. Finally, he shrugs. "Very well. Seven years' service and I'll save them."

My jaw drops. "That can't be anywhere as hard as breaking a seraph bond. Why is the cost the same?" Wolf had warned of exactly this, but part of me didn't believe him.

"I have my reasons."

I open my mouth, but I don't have a good argument. Even if I'm willing to do seven years of service—and I am—the complications presented previously still apply. The men won't like it. More, we don't know what will happen to the seraph bond if I'm whisked away to another realm. Maybe it would be okay.

Or maybe it would kill us all.

He gives that sharp smile. "I'll be back tomorrow. Have your answer by then." He casts a disdainful look at the blood-stained floor. "Next time, use my card." It appears in the air above me, floating carefully down to rest on my thigh that isn't covered in blood.

And then he's gone, melting into the shadows as if he'd never existed.

I lean my head back against the bed and sigh. No good

options. No matter what I try, there are no good options. Azazel was a long shot, but I can hand the card off to Grace. Even if we can't save my men, at least she'll get a chance to find some resolution about her mother. A small win, I suppose.

I close my eyes and concentrate on taking slow breaths. It's starting to look like I really only have one choice. If I can't stage an assault to save the men or sneak them out, there's only one path left, no matter how foolhardy it sounds.

I have to walk through the front gate and declare myself my father's heir.

4

I MANAGE TO CLEAN UP THE BLOOD BEFORE I PASS OUT again. This time, when I wake up surrounded by mist, there's no confusion. I climb to my feet, already looking for whichever one of my men waits for me. Mist swirls at my feet as I start walking, searching the opaque space for familiar forms.

When I see three of them, I almost sob. I break into a run. One step. Two. On the third, I'm among them. Malachi, with his broad shoulders and long dark hair. Rylan, who manages to look put together and vaguely annoyed despite the gaunt lines in his cheeks. And Wolf, all wild eyes and fury.

He's the one who grabs my shoulders. "You're pregnant."

The mist around us seems to dampen the sound, but the other two men go even quieter in response to his words. I don't look at them. I can't. I just give a shaky nod. "I am. I felt it the day you were taken, but I took a test to confirm."

Wolf releases me like I've burned him. "Is that why we can't feel her? I thought it was the drugs."

"It could be both." Rylan speaks from almost directly behind me. Even his voice is raspier than normal. "Not much is known about seraph pregnancy. They always disappeared during those months, and any record of it has long since been destroyed."

"You should have told us."

I turn to face Malachi, but he's not looking at me. He's looking at Rylan, his dark brows pulled together. "If there's a risk to her because of this—"

"Wake up, Malachi. There's a risk to *all* of us. She's not the one currently chained and injected with poison."

My stomach drops. "I'm getting you out." I don't tell them that I'm exhausted. That I can't seem to keep down a single bite of food. That I can't touch the well of magic inside me that only seems to get further and further from the tips of my fingers with every day that passes. All that might be true, but in the end, it's just an excuse.

They're suffering more than I am.

They have more at stake if I fail.

"No." Malachi shakes his head. "It's too dangerous. We'll figure something out."

"Like you figured out a way to escape that house?" He spent a hundred years trapped and slowly starving between sacrifices my father sent him. I can't bear the thought of him suffering through that again, let alone Rylan and Wolf, too. I glare up at him. "Out of the question."

In fact, as I look from one of them to the other, they all show marks of starvation. It shouldn't have happened this quickly; it hasn't even been a week and we all but glutted ourselves on blood before the capture. Yes, we were essentially just passing it back and forth but...

The sinking feeling in my chest gets worse. "You weren't feeding the way you needed to before this."

Suddenly Malachi won't quite meet my gaze. It's Rylan who answers, "I was." Which all but admits that the other two weren't.

I knew he'd ranged farther than Malachi and Wolf, but it hadn't occurred to me that he was effectively working as hunter for our entire group until now. It should have. I take a step back so I can see all three of them. "Feed from me." I don't know if it will work in dreams, but this isn't a normal dream or we wouldn't be able to meet like this at all. Malachi starts to shake his head and I grab his arm. "*Feed from me.* If you want me to find another way, then you need to stay alive and healthy enough to fight when I come for you." I don't know what plan I can possibly come up with on my own, but I'll say anything to decrease their current suffering.

Malachi still looks like he wants to argue. Even Wolf holds back, something serious and worried in his pale blue eyes. I know he's thinking of the last time we met like this and the information I compelled out of him.

Strangely enough, it's Rylan who steps forward. "We don't know what it will do to you. Or if it will work at all."

"Might as well try it." I have been so damn helpless from the start of this. I don't want to be helpless anymore. If I can lessen their suffering at all, even a little, I want to do that. I *need* to do that.

I tilt my head to the side. It's only then that I realize I'm still wearing the same clothes I had on when I fell asleep. It makes a strange sort of sense, but there's no time to think too hard about it because Rylan moves forward, too fast to track even for my dhampir eyes, and bites me.

I expect pleasure.

All I get is pain.

He rears back with a muffled curse, his hand to his mouth. "What the fuck was *that?*"

I drop to my knees and press my fingers to the bite. It's only two pinpricks from his canines, but the pain keeps radiating through me as if he injected poison into my blood. "What's wrong? It's never hurt before."

Rylan removes his hand and there are burn marks on his lips. He shakes his head. "It has to be the pregnancy."

"Or it's this realm." Malachi studies the space above us, though it doesn't look any different from what's around us in every direction. "I'm not prepared to blame the baby. We don't know enough to say for sure."

"For fuck's sake, Malachi, no one is blaming that thing." Rylan swipes his hand across his mouth again, as if he wants to scrub the taste of me right off his tongue. No reason for that to sting, but my logical side isn't online right now. He shakes his head. "Something's off, and it has nothing to do with this realm, if it's even a realm. She might have simply pulled us into her dreams."

"Which means the blood you just consumed isn't really blood." Malachi sounds calm. Too calm. "It might be the seraph bond attempting to protect her when she's already weakened. We won't know until we're back together in person."

"When that happens, *you* can bite her first."

I prop my hands on my hips and glare. "I'm standing right here. Stop talking about me like I'm a child."

Malachi and Rylan both look away, expressions sheepish and irritated in turn. Which is when Wolf speaks. "Did you make a deal, love?"

The breath whooshes out of my body. He's been so uncharacteristically quiet, I almost convinced myself he wouldn't speak about what happened before. I should know better by now. There are few secrets between the four of us, at least when it comes to current events. The past is another animal entirely.

I make myself meet his gaze steadily. "Not yet."

Malachi whips around. "What the fuck is he talking about? What deal?"

"I can explain. I—"

Wolf speaks right over me. "She asked me how to summon Azazel. When I refused to tell her, she compelled me."

I don't like the betrayed look Rylan sends my way. Even worse is the slow anger building on Malachi's face. He drags his hands through his long hair. "We talked about this, Mina. It's out of the question."

"It was out of the question before my father took you three. It's not now." I'm protesting mostly out of spite, though. I can't accept Azazel's bargain now any more than I could before. I sigh. "Look, I'm not taking the deal. I thought he'd give different terms, but he didn't, so we're back to square one. If any of you have any brilliant ideas, I'd love to hear it."

They exchange a look, but no one says anything. I don't

know whether to laugh or cry. The three of them have gotten me out of several messes to date. I can't expect them to do it when they're captive and I'm free. "I'll find another way." I swallow hard, a burning starting in my throat and eyes. "I won't bargain away seven years. I promise."

They don't quite look like they believe me, but that's fine. I deserve the distrust after compelling Wolf. It was the wrong call, but panic got the best of me. That's no excuse, and I won't try to make it one. I lift my chin and open my mouth, but my stomach gives a horrible surge of agony that has me doubling over. "No. It's too soon."

"Mina!" Malachi's hand brushes my back and then he's gone, jerked away into the mist as if a giant hand reached out and snatched him. By the time I look for Rylan and Wolf, they've disappeared as well.

I barely get to curse before the world goes dark. The pain follows me into my waking, cramps that bow my back and have me clamping my teeth shut to keep a scream internal. This time, there's no Grace to help. I turn onto my side and pull my knees to my chest. It feels like something is gnawing away at my insides, dull teeth ripping and tearing and gods, it hurts. It hurts so fucking bad.

Until it doesn't.

I blink through my watering eyes. I can't keep from locking my body, waiting for the next wave of pain. It takes me much longer than I want to admit to slowly unclench and cautiously stretch out my legs. I half expect to find something wrong, but the pain has faded as if it never existed.

But like last time, I'm covered in sweat and feel shaky.

I stagger to the bathroom and take a quick shower, feeling

dizzy all the while. By the time I make it back into the bedroom to pull on the jeans and a T-shirt Grace sourced for me from the local thrift store, I'm almost feeling like myself again.

Well, like the new version of myself who's weak and exhausted and vaguely nauseous at all times.

At least there are no bite marks on my neck, which seems to suggest that Malachi was right about the seraph bond trying to protect me in that dreamy place. I shouldn't take it personally that my blood might be poisonous to my men, but I don't like the thought at all. I enjoy their bites, and not simply for the orgasm that inevitably follows. Exchanging blood has become an intimacy that I don't want to give up.

I glare down at my stomach. "You are a giant pain in the ass."

"Talking to yourself is generally frowned upon." Grace strides through the door and shuts it behind her. She looks as tired as I feel, circles beneath her eyes and her hair escaping its braid. She raises her eyebrows at me. "You look like shit."

"I was just about to say the same thing about you."

She shrugs. "Nothing more than the truth." Grace drops onto the bed across from me. "I don't suppose you have good news? Because all I have is bad."

"Tell me." I have a feeling she's going to get sidetracked as soon as I tell her about Azazel. Beyond that, I've always been one who prefers the bite of bad news before the soothing of good news. My life has had little of the latter until recently and certainly not enough to get used to it.

"He's upped patrols from when you were last there. There are fewer gaps in his security than expected. There was also a large group of vampires who arrived today who seemed to be new, or at least not locals, based on how they were received."

He's pulling in his people. I should have expected as much, but it seems like such overkill, at least until I consider the value and strength of his captives. My father will be taking no risks with them. He wants them locked down and he'll do whatever he has to in order to ensure it. "Well, shit."

"Pretty much." She pins me with a long look. "What happened while I was gone?" She keeps talking before I have a chance to respond. "Don't bother to lie and say nothing happened because I know it did. There are blood stains on the floor and there's still magic lingering in the air."

I glance guiltily at the floor. "I thought I got it all." Wait a damn minute. I whip around to look at her. "Since when can you see magic?" Now that I think about it, she mentioned something about it before, but I was too rattled from that first dream with Wolf to notice.

"Since always. Old family trick. Which is why I know you're not anything as simple as a dhampir, though I'm not going to pry on *that*. This?" She makes a circle with her finger to encompass the room. "Different story. You went into your dreams with those vampires again, didn't you? But there's something else."

I drag in a breath. There's no point in hiding the truth from her. If I can't utilize Azazel, as least I can ensure she's able to contact him. "I summoned the demon."

5

GRACE SURPRISES ME. INSTEAD OF PRACTICALLY TACK-ling me to get more information, she pulls a sleeve of crackers out of her purse, hands them over, and waits until I tentatively nibble on one to start questioning me. "You summoned Azazel."

"Yes. I tried the blood circle and it failed miserably, but he ended up showing up anyways." I haven't had a chance to think about that too closely, which was likely best. I can't imagine Azazel noticed every time someone says his name. It isn't common, but statistically *someone* had to use it occasionally in a way that had nothing to do with summoning the demon himself, which meant he was either close or he's keeping an eye on me. Maybe he was hoping I'd change my mind about the original bargain and try to summon him without my men around.

The thought isn't comforting in the least.

Another thing to add to the list of worries. I don't *think* Azazel can force me to agree, but he seems overly invested in it. Maybe it's just to mess with Wolf, but I can't take anything for granted now. Maybe the demon simply has a quota of deals to meet. The thought is strangely hilarious.

"Mina."

"Sorry. Right." I shake my head, trying to focus. "He said he could help with getting Malachi, Rylan, and Wolf out, but he won't budge on the terms of the bargain. It's seven years' service in another realm." I sigh. "I can't risk it. It's not even about time moving differently. It's about the bond. It might just flat-out kill all four of us, which kind of defeats the purpose of rescuing them in the first place."

It takes several long moments before I realize Grace hasn't responded. I look over to find her staring off into the middle distance. "Grace?"

"Just thinking," she says slowly. "Did you reject the bargain?"

"He's coming tomorrow to collect his answer." It speaks of long experience that he gives his marks time to consider the offer. It's easy enough to reject something with such a high cost, but given enough time to realize how few options you have? Seven years begins to sound much more reasonable. "It's not going to matter. I might be willing to pay the price of time, but I won't pay with our lives."

"We'll think of something." She still sounds strange, distant, as if her mind if jumping forward a thousand times faster than mine.

Considering how woozy I feel, that's not saying much. I finish my cracker and set the package down, waiting for my stomach to decide if it will hold. I don't have high hopes. Nothing stays down. I press my hand to my neck where Rylan bit me in the dream. It doesn't feel any different, but I can't get the memory out of my head. Even if my blood didn't suddenly become poisonous, my vampires won't agree to drink from me when they see how haggard I look. I hardly have blood to spare at this point.

"We keep saying that, but no solutions are magically appearing." I look down at my stomach. If I had my magic under control… If I could even access it…

Then I think about how fierce Malachi was at the thought of my being pregnant. That was before it even happened. I press my hand to my stomach. If I lose them… My brain tries to shy away from the thought, but I force myself to power through. If I lose them, this baby might be my only connection to them.

Selfish thought. Horrible in so many ways. I still can't shake it.

I squint at the sky lightening through the cracks in the curtains. "What time is it?"

"Early. Five."

Five? I slept through the night, even if I hardly feel rested at all. That seems to be happening more often than it's not. No matter how many hours I sleep, I still wake exhausted. I shake my head slowly. "Wait a minute. It's tomorrow. That means Azazel—"

The lights go out.

"Fuck!" Grace scrambles for the lamp on the nightstand between our beds. It clicks, but the light doesn't come on. "What the hell?"

"Little hunter." Azazel's voice seems to come from everywhere and nowhere at the same time. I twist, trying to see, but even a vampire needs a little light to see. A dhampir needs more yet, and there is none to be had in this room.

"Little seraph." His breath tickles the shell of my ear. "Did you think to trap me?"

Fear surges through me. Azazel has always been scary, but it's nothing compared to what he is now. I try to swallow past the need to scream. "No. No one's trying to trap you."

"And yet you are here with *her*."

"Not for that!" I can't guarantee Grace isn't here for *that*. She's overly interested in Azazel and has good reason to be. She wants answers about her mother. Would she try to kill him, even if it meant I failed?

I don't know.

"Do you know what I do to people who try to cross me?"

I can't move, can't think. Panic bleats through me, as worthless as the ever-present exhaustion weighing me down. It builds and builds, a rising tide that washes away all rational thought. "*Stop!*"

Flames lick at the air around me, Malachi's power manifesting out of my pure desperation. The flames are nowhere near as strong as I've summoned in the past, but they're enough to break the unrelenting dark. I get a glimpse of a monster crouching behind Grace, massive shoulders and arms, horns like a bull coming from either side of its head.

No, not it.

Him.

Azazel.

My flames go out, but this time the darkness only lasts a moment. The light at the bedside table flickers on, weakly doing battle with the shadows seeming to gather in every corner of the room. And there Azazel is, once again wearing his human skin, standing at the space between the ends of our beds, his hands in the pockets of his slacks. His eyes flare red, not quite managing to keep things under wraps. "Explain yourselves. Quickly."

There's no explicit threat tacked onto the end of that sentence, but there doesn't need to be. It hangs in the air, thicker than smoke.

I exchange a look with Grace. She seems shaken but determined in a way that does nothing to reassure me. If she attacks Azazel, neither of us will survive the next few minutes. "Don't do anything foolish," I snap.

Her gaze flicks my way and she tenses. "You took my mother."

"I don't take people. I make deals." He sounds bored. His tone is a lie. From the careful way he holds himself, he's half a breath from attacking us. He turns his attention to me. "I'll have your answer now."

All this mess and I feel like I'm just digging in further. I can't say yes. I'm not sure what he'll do if I say no. "I—"

"I'd like to propose a new bargain," Grace cuts in.

Azazel's interest sharpens on her. "How forward of you."

"I'm just that kind of girl." Her smile is a challenge. "You help Mina get her men back. I'll pay the price."

He sighs. "What do you think you can offer that would replace a half seraph? You're hardly a catch, darling."

"Don't call me darling." She straightens. "I'm the last of the Cel Tradat family. I might only be human, but that means something, even to a monster like you. My family has a long history with the people of your realm. Don't try to pretend securing me in a bargain isn't a coup."

"Calling me names is not the way to get what you want." He

stalks forward, darkness flowing around him. It's enough for me to realize how tightly leashed he kept himself up to this point. He's not even trying now, though he's managed to get control of his form. Either that or there's not enough light for his shadow to betray him.

"Mina won't accept your deal. I will. That already makes me the better bet."

"Hmm." He glances at me, expression shuttered. "You're probably more trouble that you're worth at this point. Not to mention I'll have to suffer through Wolf attempting to summon me repeatedly to demand you back." Azazel shakes his head. "Very well, let's discuss terms."

I can't tell whether Grace looks victorious or sick to her stomach. She lifts her chin. "Rescue Malachi, Rylan, and Wolf, and kill Mina's father in the process. Then I'll go with you."

He chuckles, the sound low and unamused. "You presume you're worth that much, last Cel Tradat or no. Pick one." He pauses. "And you will pay up front."

That snaps me out of my daze. "No. You're not going to take her before you rescue them." *Seven years* under my father's tender care? Unacceptable. "You should rescue them simply because Wolf is a friend."

"I'm a demon, little seraph. I don't have friends."

"How sad for you." Grace shakes her head. "But she's right. What's the point in saving them if they're broken by the time you do? That's a shitty deal."

"Ladies." He sighs again, even more exasperated this time. "I'm under a deadline and I don't have the luxury of this song and dance. I will fulfill my end of the bargain within twenty-four hours of time here. The lovely...Grace...will leave now and come to my realm to fulfill her seven years."

I want to be relieved, but I can't. I *can't*. Too many people are paying debts that should be mine. I press my hands hard to my thighs and look at Grace. "You can't accept. You don't even know what you're walking into. I don't care if..." I hesitate. I doubt Azazel is ignorant of the fact that he made a deal with Grace's mother, but if by some miracle he is, I'm not going to be the one to out her. I clear my throat. "You can't pay this price for us. The cost is too high."

"I'm not doing it for you." She says it firmly but not unkindly. "No offense, but I wouldn't pay this price unless I wanted to."

There will be no reasoning with her, then. I turn to the demon. "I want assurances that she won't be harmed or killed, not by your hand or anyone in that realm. If you can't ensure her safety and comfort, she's not saying yes."

"Mina—"

It's hard to be certain, but I think Azazel actually rolls his eyes. "If you weren't so busy throwing out accusations, I would have already laid out the terms in detail. There are formalities to a demon bargain, after all."

"If you try to trick her—"

"Your opinion of me is truly staggering." He shakes his head. "In three days, you will be auctioned off to one of the leaders of the territories in my realm. You will agree to serve them in what- ever way they need, but they will not harm, hurt, or otherwise mistreat you, under pain of death."

I narrow my eyes. "How can you guarantee that? If they harm her, even if they pay a price afterward, she's still harmed."

"I'm a *demon*. My bargains have meanings." He sounds so exasperated, I almost forget to be scared. Almost.

"Serve them in whatever way they need," Grace repeats. "You want me to fuck demons."

"You will not be coerced against your will."

She snorts. "Nice dodge, but by agreeing to this bargain, I'm agreeing to the sex."

Azazel speaks through gritted teeth. "You will allow them the chance to seduce you, but they cannot force you. To do so would qualify as harm."

It sounds like a sneaky loophole from where I'm sitting. I'm about to say as much when Grace shrugs. "Fine. I agree."

"Wait!"

"Perfect." He offers his hand. "We seal it with a kiss."

"Grace, no."

But it's too late. She slips her hand into his. He raises it to his mouth, flips it, and presses a kiss to her wrist. A mark blooms there, black and red, painting itself across her tanned skin in a pattern that seems to shift in a way that defies comprehension.

Azazel glances at me without releasing Grace. "I'll return to pay my end of the bargain tomorrow. Stay out of trouble until then."

Darkness surges and I throw up my hand to cover my eyes. One blink and the room is empty except for me, the shadows returning to the normal faded ones from early morning.

Grace is gone.

Fuck.

6

I SPEND THE NEXT TWENTY-FOUR HOURS IN MISERY. I still can't keep anything down and I'm so tired, I don't bother to leave the motel room. Thankfully, I don't have to. Grace paid through the end of the week, so at least I don't have to be worried about being kicked out.

Another price she paid on my behalf.

It doesn't matter if she said she was doing it for herself, if she accepted Azazel's bargain because she was looking for answers about her mother. She never would have had access to the demon in the first place if not for me. If anything horrible happens to her…The fact that she just lost *seven years*…

Everyone is making sacrifices for me. Malachi. Rylan. Wolf. Now Grace, who's little more than a stranger. Meanwhile, I'm huddled here on a motel bed, waiting to be rescued. Again. It's enough to make me want to scream.

I feel the change in the air before Azazel materializes in front of me. It's a strange sort of static electricity, like right before a lightning storm. One moment the room is mundane and ordinary, and the next shadows reign supreme despite the relative early hour.

I won't say Azazel's less scary after all these interactions, but I don't have the energy to cower right now. I just blink up at him as he towers over me. "Took you long enough." Even my voice sounds wrong. Weak and thready.

He frowns. "What's the matter with you?"

"Just special, I guess."

He frowns harder and leans down to coast his hand over my body. He doesn't touch me, keeping a careful few inches of distance between us, but it still feels too intimate. Especially when he hovers over my midsection and huffs out a laugh. "I suppose that would do it. You're cooking quite the little beast in there, aren't you?"

"Don't call them a little beast." The words rush out before I can think. I might have more than a little resentment about the pregnancy, but that doesn't mean I'm going to let this demon talk about the...baby...like that.

"If you insist." His dark brows draw together, eyes lighting almost red for a moment. "Ah, I see. That would do it."

"What are you talking about?" I don't like this. I'm prone and feel particularly helpless, and he hasn't moved his hand away from my stomach. "Back off."

"Your shields are abysmal."

"I'm aware," I grit out. I can't sit up because he still hasn't moved and I don't want to risk accidentally touching him, but I don't like this. Not a single bit. "Get away from me. I mean it." I try to inject as much authority into my voice as possible. I don't know what I'll do if he doesn't listen. I don't know what I *can* do.

"I'm feeling generous after meeting my quota so I'll help you out for free." He presses a single finger against my lower stomach in the gap between my T-shirt and my jeans. It's such a tiny touch. A single fingertip. It still goes through me like a giant bell tolling. The room gives a sickening spin and then another and another before finally settling back into place.

"What the fuck? I told you—" I stop short. I feel different. Lighter. Like I can draw a full breath for the first time in over a week. I'd attributed that claustrophobic feeling to worry about my men, but it was the pregnancy all along? I narrow my eyes at the demon standing over me. "What did you do?"

"Supplemental shield. It won't stop the beast from growing or gaining the necessary sustenance to survive, but it will stop the constant drain of power." He considers. "Think of it as a funnel rather than a waterfall. Better for both of you, I imagine."

"Do you have a lot of experience with seraph pregnancies and the resulting vampire-hybrid babies?" I manage.

"You'd be surprised."

"Can you—"

"You already got this for free. Don't press your luck asking for more." He straightens abruptly. "I'll retrieve your vampires once it reaches full dark. Where do you want them?" He makes a show of looking around. "This place is hardly secure and your father will be searching for them."

I finally sit up. He's still too close, his shadows taking up too much space and making him seem larger than his human form. It's disconcerting in the extreme. "You took seven years of Grace's life and you can't even guarantee that you won't leave a trail for them to follow?"

He sighs. "You continue to press me. It's irritating."

A few weeks ago, having a ridiculously powerful and scary demon exasperated with me would be enough for common sense to take over and silence me. No longer. I lift my chin. "Then maybe you should make better deals. You're supposed to be so powerful. My father is just a vampire. What's that compared to a demon?"

Azazel sighs again, louder. "Fine." He produces a card from somewhere and passes it over. It looks nearly identical to the one from earlier, except it has an address on it. "That's a one-way ticket, so don't use it until you're ready to go."

"Go," I repeat.

He doesn't roll his eyes, but it looks like he wants to. "Yes, *go*. When you're prepared to leave, hold it to your chest and concentrate. Anything you're carrying will be transported with you."

A sliver of cold works its way through me. Teleportation. Obviously, I knew Azazel could do it since he seems to come and go as he pleases, but to allow someone else to do it independently of him? The thought makes me shudder. It seems risky. Surely there are a thousand things that could go wrong while I'm a disembodied version of myself, winging from one location to another. If that's even how teleportation works. I honestly have no idea.

Riskier than trying to call a cab and leaving a trail for some-one to follow if they know where to look?

No. Not riskier than that.

I finally nod. "It will be safe there?"

"Safe enough." He shrugs. "What happens after that is up to the four of you. My help ends with the transfer."

He looks like he's about to leave, but I find myself speaking before he can pull a disappearing act. "Azazel."

He waits, eyes dark and far too knowing. It would be so easy to let fear silence me, but I breathe through it and say, "If Grace is hurt because of the deal she made with you, I'll find a way to kill you myself." Maybe it's an impossible task, but I'll do what I can to repay that debt.

His lips curve, though his eyes remain cold. "As long as she follows the rules, she'll be fine."

If Grace finds out someone in that realm was the reason her mother never returned, she might murder them. Or at least try. I don't know her well enough to know for sure. Maybe she'll try to kill Azazel himself. The thought has me fighting back another shiver. "She made that deal because of me."

"If you say so. Seems like she was intent on it for her own purposes." He cocks his head to the side as if listening to some-thing I can't hear. "Don't linger here. They'll be searching the area shortly." Then he's gone, sinking into the shadows on the floor as if stepping into a deep pool of water. It's more disconcert-ing than when he just disappears in a flood of darkness.

I test the floor, now clear of shadows, and it feels solid enough. "Creepy."

I don't know what to think of Azazel's *supplemental shield*, but it's a worry for another day. At this point, I have a *lot* of worries for later dates. There's no help for it. I need to gather what few things I have and get out of here. The card feels strange against my palm, a faint pulse coming from it.

Teleportation.

I shouldn't be surprised that it's possible. In the last couple weeks, I've seen plenty of things that I'd previously thought impossible. With all that said, this feels particularly fantastical. I shake my head and make quick work of packing up anything that could link me to this room. There's the blood on the floor, but I can't do much about that without burning the place down, and I'm not willing to do that. My father isn't able to track from some old blood.

Even he was, he wouldn't have to tear up the carpet in this hotel room to have access to my blood. I left plenty of it behind in his compound over the years, originating with one punishment or another. I shake off the dark thoughts and throw the last few things in my bag.

My gaze tracks to the desk where Grace's weapons are laid out. I can't leave them. When we spoke about deals, Azazel made it sound like time moved differently in the other realm, so seven years might pass in a matter of months or even days. If Grace returns that quickly on our side of things, I want her to have her weapons. It's the absolute least I can do.

As I carefully pack them into the duffel bag she'd brought in, I notice a few of the knives are missing. Two daggers and one that's long enough to be a short sword. I laughed when I first saw it and asked her if she planned on fighting any Spartans. She hadn't been amused.

I didn't even see her grab them during that short conversation with Azazel before she made her deal. Maybe she'd already had them on her. Or maybe she was better at sleight of hand than I could have imagined. I press my lips together. *I hope you know what you're getting into.*

After slinging both bags over my shoulders, I grab the card and examine it. He said I just need to concentrate, which sounds deceptively simple. Everything about magic is deceptively simple.

Just reach for it.

Just imagine what you want it to do.

Just let it do what it's meant to do.

I snort and press the card to my chest. Nothing happens. Of course nothing happens. Why would anything magical I attempt actually work on the first try? I take a slow breath and close my eyes. The desire to leave, to see my men again, whole and healthy, slams into me so hard, it makes me dizzy. I choke on a ragged inhale and the world seems to go sickeningly liquid for half a beat.

When I open my eyes, I'm somewhere else.

I turn a slow circle, taking in the relatively normal living room I now stand in. It looks like something out of a sitcom. Small and cozy with furniture that has a lived-in kind of feel. A staircase leads up to the second floor and I can see the kitchen through the doorway in the back of the room. Another turn shows what appears to be a front door.

The bags go on the low coffee table. I pad to the front door to peer out the windows on either side. I'd half expected to find a street with rows of nearly identical houses, but there is only a gravel driveway leading down a hill into dark trees. Not a single light breaks up the growing darkness, though in the distance I can see what appears to be a town. I exhale slowly. Good. With this house being so isolated, it means there's less chance of innocents getting caught in the crossfire if my father's people find us again.

Less chances of close neighbors asking questions about weird sights and sounds, too.

I do a quick search of the house, but there's nothing worth noting. A few bedrooms with large beds, a deceptively nice shower, a modern kitchen with a fridge and pantry packed with food. I pause there, considering. My stomach is cramping with hunger and I feel a little woozy, but I have energy for the first time since I found out I was pregnant. "Maybe this supplemental shield will help with the morning sickness?" I murmur.

Ten minutes later, I have my answer as I puke up the few crackers I managed to choke down. Damn it.

I drag myself to the living room to dig out my toothbrush so I can scrub the taste out of my mouth. That done, I circle back to the fridge. Food is right out, but I had seen some electrolyte-packed drinks in there. Maybe that will help.

A thud from the living room has me spinning around.

I rush through the doorway to find Azazel standing over my three men as if he just dumped them in a pile. Azazel brushes his hands together as if dusting them off. "Good luck." Then he disappears in a surge of shadows.

I don't hesitate. I drop my drink and rush toward the men. "Are you okay?"

Malachi is at the bottom of the pile, but he throws up a hand. "Stop."

I freeze a few feet away. "What?"

"We're..." He shakes his head, eyes slightly unfocused. His handsome face is haggard and drawn, cheekbones stark. "Not safe."

What they said in the last dream comes rushing back. Somehow my father managed to get them to the brink of starvation in only a few days. In all the chaos, I hadn't had much time to think about it. Now, the truth stares me right in the face, evidence blatant in the fact that all three of them have obviously lost weight. Too much weight. More, they're too pale, their skin stretched tight over their bones. Even Malachi's long hair seems dull and brittle.

I don't move, but I don't retreat, either. "You need blood."

"Not yours," Rylan grinds out. He lifts his head and the gauntness of his cheeks makes my stomach drop. "Need too much."

They can't go hunting like this. They can barely move. If they don't trust me to touch them—or, rather, don't trust themselves to allow me close—then I'll have to hunt for them. The thought fills me with unease, but I'll do anything to keep my men safe. If that means someone else has to pay the price...

Well, it's becoming something of a trend, isn't it?

It's so much easier to make that call for them than it is for myself, though. I would commit unforgivable acts to keep my men with me and safe. I spent a lot of time pretending I'm not just as monstrous as my father, but in this moment, I don't even hesitate. I take a slow step back. "Stay here."

"Mina."

I hold Malachi's gaze. "Stay here. I'll be back."

"*Mina.*"

I don't give him a chance to argue. I spin on my heel and rush back into the kitchen. I had noticed a hook with keys on it by the back door. Sure enough, outside, I find a tiny garage with a truck parked there. It even has a full tank of gas. "Thanks, Azazel," I mutter.

I don't have much experience with driving, but I won't let that stop me. The clock reads midnight as I tear out of the garage and kick up gravel behind me. At this time of night, there's only one option for scoping out victims.

I need to find a bar.

7

I DON'T KNOW WHAT STATE AZAZEL TRANSPORTED US to. I couldn't guess the name of the midsize town I drive into under pain of death. But I manage to find a pair of bars before too long. I park and study them. One is a dive bar with a faded sign that's completely unreadable in the deepening dark, even to my dhampir eyes. The other is newer and already has a crowd of people on the patio surrounded by dangling white string lights.

That'll do.

I glance down at myself. I didn't pause to put myself together before leaving the house—or the motel. My jeans are faded and I've started to wear holes in the knees. My black T-shirt is clean, but with how tired I look, I won't be winning any beauty contests.

How am I supposed to convince people to come with me? How am I supposed to *choose*?

If Malachi doesn't trust himself to drink from me, he must be famished. Rylan and Wolf were no better. There's a decent chance whatever human I bring back to the house will never leave again. That I'll be sentencing whoever I pick to death.

I grip the steering wheel and exhale slowly. I knew the cost when I came here. Waffling and feeling guilty won't change anything. If it's the choice between the men I love or a few strangers? I already know where I stand. It's not moral and it's not right, but I can't bring myself to care. I have not come this far, allowed so much sacrifice, only to balk now.

In the end, it's so much easier than I would have thought.

No one asks for my ID when I walk through the door. Inside is much like the outside: vaguely trendy and ultimately soulless. I could be anywhere. The tables and bar are packed, but everyone seems to be sticking to groups rather than mingling as a whole. I can work with this…I think.

I find a spot at the corner of the bar and order a beer on tap because it's the cheapest thing on the menu. The smell makes my stomach twist, but I force myself to wrap my hands around the glass and take a deep breath. I can do this. I don't have a choice. I just need a moment to figure out a plan.

I don't get a chance.

Two men slide up on either side of me. Too close. I might not be human and even I know that. They're almost touching me, their bodies angled in almost like they're attempting to pin me between them without touching me. They both look rough around the edges, and the alcohol on their breath is even stronger than the scent wafting from the beer in front of me.

I tense. "You're standing too close."

"Haven't seen you around here before, beautiful," the one on the left says. He's got a voice like he smokes a pack a day. He certainly reeks of tobacco.

I half turn to face him. If I were human, I would have missed the movement of his friend at my back. I never would have seen him drop a tablet into my beer. It disappears almost immediately, fizzling out as it descends to the bottom of the glass. It happened *so fast*. Fast enough to make me suspect they've done this before.

The guilt I've harbored since leaving my men behind disintegrates. I'm not one to play judge, jury, and executioner to humans, but if these two think to play predator, I'll show them they aren't the scariest thing in this bar.

It's pathetically easy to pretend to drink the beer. Really, the most challenging part is not throwing up from the scent of it. Halfway through, I let myself list a little to the side. Mr. Right Side is there to catch me, sliding a beefy arm around my waist. "Looks like someone's had too much."

Mr. Left Side chuckles. "Better see her safely home." He even goes so far as to pay for my beer. *What a gentleman.* The bartender gives them a knowing look, which only serves to set my teeth on edge. They *have* done this before. I'd stake my life on it. I mostly keep my feet, but I force myself to half limp, letting them take my weight.

I understand the bartender's look a few minutes later when they haul me out of the bar and we find him waiting around back. He brushes his hands off on his pants. "Let's make this quick. I only have fifteen minutes."

I don't feel guilty at all as I strike.

I might be no match for Malachi and Rylan and Wolf in the sparring ring, but these three are only human. They barely have time to react before I deliver harsh blows to their temples. Not quite enough to kill them—at least I don't think so—but they go down in boneless heaps.

"You fuckers," I spit on the ground. I want to kick them a few times for good measure but if the bartender only had fifteen minutes to get up to no good, then I have fewer than that before someone comes looking for him.

I hurry to the truck and drive it around back. All three of them are still unconscious as I toss their bodies into the bed of the truck and get out of there as quickly and quietly as possible. The drive back to the house seems to take forever, but at least it's easy enough to remember the route.

As I take the dirt road toward the house, I wait for guilt to sweep over me. I didn't hesitate. Even if they hadn't been trying to hurt me, I would have let them think they'd seduced me into going home with them. The end result would be the same. I get no points just because they turned out to be rotten to the core.

The guilt never comes.

Malachi and the other two are nearly exactly where I left them. They've separated a bit, but they don't seem to have the strength to even climb onto the couches. A sliver of fear goes through me but I don't pause long enough to indulge in it. They *have* to be okay. I can't let myself go down a mental road where they aren't. Once they feed, they'll feel better. I'm sure of it. "We're going to stain the rug, but there's no help for it."

Wolf cracks his eyes open. "What did you do, love?"

"What I needed to." No point in explaining beyond that. I go back outside and start hauling the unconscious men inside. It's only as I dump the final unconscious man next to Malachi that I register the fact that I haven't felt the need for a nap since arriving at this house. Before this point, I was taking three naps a day, sleeping more than I was awake. I've been going for hours and still feel relatively fresh.

Apparently Azazel was onto something with that supplemental shield, though I'll be damned before I admit as much to him. If I ever see him again, that is. It's probably better if I don't.

Though I half expect the men to continue questioning me, hunger prevails. Wolf moves first, grabbing the bartender and biting deep. The man groans softly but doesn't stir. Good. It's one thing to attack them when they intended to attack me first. I don't know how I'd feel about them struggling and begging for their lives now.

Then again, these are bloodline vampires we're talking about. Their bites bring great pleasure. After that first contact, no one is fighting anything. They're too busy riding the waves of desire and begging for more.

I certainly was.

It takes less time than one would expect to drain a human body of blood. By the end of it, we have three corpses and all three men look much closer to themselves. I am almost convinced I can see their faces start to look healthier, their gauntness melting away.

Malachi surges to his feet and pulls me into his arms. "Are you hurt?"

My laugh feels a little broken. I'm not the one who has spent nearly a week in my father's not so tender care. I might be permanently nauseous, but the worst I've had to deal with is Grace being cranky in the mornings and throwing up everything I eat. Small things by comparison. "I'm better off than you were."

"Azazel—"

"I'm not the one who paid the price," I cut in. I twist to see Rylan climbing to his feet, almost human slow. "Grace did. She chose it."

He sighs. "I was worried that would happen once I realized who Wolf was summoning. Her mother and Azazel have a history. I thought I could keep the knowledge from her, but this outcome was always likely."

"Who did you *think* I was summoning?" Wolf brushes his hands down his thighs. "There are only so many demons who can cross into our realm and you know it. I can count them on one hand, and half of them haven't been seen in a hundred years."

"Likely because Azazel killed them to corner the market for himself."

"Maybe." Wolf shrugs. He turns to me, uncharacteristically serious. "We're going to get rid of these bodies and then it's time to talk, love."

Malachi's arms tighten around me. "Yes."

They're right that we need to talk, but that doesn't make me look forward to the pending conversation more. There's no strange misty place to sweep us apart when things get awkward, and things are *guaranteed* to get awkward. I compelled Wolf against his will and then I summoned Azazel even though they told me not to. That's not even getting into the whole pregnancy thing.

At least we're back together again. We haven't made any progress with removing the threat my father poses, but he no long has access to three bloodline vampires. To three men I love.

I shiver and Malachi pulls me closer yet. "Sit down, little dhampir. We'll deal with this. You've done enough for now."

It doesn't feel like I've done much of anything at all. I ran when they were captured. I let Grace do all the heavy lifting of recon and surveying my father's compound while I puked up my guts in the motel room. I couldn't even summon Azazel correctly. And then *Grace* paid the price of my bargain. Gods, I even needed Azazel to do some kind of special ward to keep the pregnancy from draining me dry.

I've never felt more worthless in my life. A feat, that. After growing up a powerless dhampir in my father's compound, I didn't think I could sink to lower depths. Apparently I was too optimistic.

But there's no time for self-pity. "I can help."

"You *have* helped." He lets me step away from him, though he runs his hands down my arms and links his fingers through mine. Malachi frowns. "You've lost weight."

"So have you." A deflection, and not even a good one at that. He frowns harder. "Mina."

Wolf and Rylan stalk back through the door. They're moving better now, quickly, less humanlike. It's almost enough to convince myself the last week didn't happen. I know better, though. I step away from Malachi and sink onto the couch. There's not so much as a blood stain on the floor. *Waste not, want not.* I swallow down a hysterical giggle. Shock. It's just shock.

"Don't feel guilty, love." Wolf drops down next to me and throws his arm across the couch at my back. "Humans live so few years. We cut their lives a bit short, but they were always going to be short."

"I don't feel guilty." Not for their deaths. I would wager a small fortune that those three have harmed more people than I care to think about. Now they won't harm anyone ever again. That said, I'm not overly keen on Wolf's blasé attitude. "I might live one of those short mortal life spans. Should we just kill me right now and get it over with?"

"You won't." Rylan perches on the coffee table across from me, close enough that his knees press against mine.

Malachi takes the spot on my other side. For the first time, bracketed in by my men, I can finally breathe again. My voice goes wobbly. "I was so worried about you."

"You got us out," Rylan says, blue eyes direct. "Now tell us exactly how and everything that happened in the meantime."

It takes longer than it should. My ridiculous urge to cry only gets stronger with each point I relay, but their presence gets me through it. By the time I finish, Rylan hasn't so much as moved, Malachi is cursing quietly under his breath, and Wolf's eyes are flickering crimson.

I clear my throat. "Stop it. All of you. You look like you want to comfort *me* and I'm not the one who spent the last week starved and tortured." The starved point is blatant, but I know my father well enough to know the latter is true as well. With three new toys to play with and break, he wouldn't have been able to resist.

"Sound like you've been plenty starved," Malachi rumbles. "We fucked up, Mina. I'm sorry. You never should have been left alone."

Rylan looks away, something akin to guilt shifting over his handsome features. "I shouldn't have left. My overconfidence meant you weren't protected. I—"

My chest goes hot and tight. "No. We're not doing this. We're not going to play self-recrimination and passing the blame around. If it wasn't my fault, then it wasn't your fault, either. My father outplayed us. Now we have to make sure he doesn't get a chance to do it again." I drag in a breath. "We can't keep running. He'll just catch us again and then we'll be right back where we started." Without Grace to act as convenient willing victim and pay my debts for me. I straighten a bit, feeling grounded for the first time since, well, everything. "We have to strike before he has a chance to regroup."

8

"WE'LL TALK ABOUT OUR NEXT STEPS TOMORROW."
Malachi doesn't give me a chance to respond before he sweeps
me up and turns a slow circle. "Where are the bedrooms?"

Maybe I should argue, but the truth is I'm crashing fast and
I want to spend some time just existing with them. Azazel prom-
ised we'd be safe here, and while I'm not naive enough to expect
that to be true indefinitely, it should be true tonight at least. I
don't even think we're in the same state.

I point at the stairs. "Up."

It's not until Malachi sets me on the bed that I realize Wolf
and Rylan aren't with us. Where did they—

"Ensuring the bodies are never found."

I startle. "I forgot about the mind reading thing." It was still
so new before my father showed up, I'd barely come to terms

with the fact that the men could glean my thoughts since I never learned how to shield. Speaking of... I press my hand to my stomach. "Azazel said my lack of shields were why the pregnancy was draining me so much. He did something, and I feel better, but it's hard to trust him. He said it was a supplemental shield, but I don't know enough to verify it."

Malachi pokes his head into the door leading into what I assume is a bathroom and then comes back to the bed. He takes my hand and tugs me to my feet. "Let's shower."

"Don't tell me you're trying to conserve water." My joke falls flat as he leads me into the bathroom.

"No." He turns on the shower and faces me. "You haven't talked about the pregnancy. Everything else, but not that."

My hand drifts to my stomach but I drop it before it makes contact. "I don't know what to think. It feels like I've been barreling toward this goal, but now that we've accomplished it—or started to, or whatever—it feels unreal. I don't know how I feel." I should feel something, shouldn't I? The people on the compound who'd become pregnant treated it as a rapturous experience that was both deeply emotional and spiritual, right from the moment they realized they'd conceived.

I don't feel anything at all.

"Mina." Malachi cups my chin gently and lifts my face until I meet his gaze. His handsome face is oh so serious, dark eyes intense. "I know we thought this was the only way, but if you don't want this, we'll find a different option."

"Just like that?" The question catches in my throat and comes out jagged. "You told me you couldn't wait to knock me up."

"I know." He shrugs, though his intensity doesn't waver. "But I care about you more than anything else, little dhampir. If you don't want children, then we won't have children."

That's the thing. I don't know what I want. I can barely think about a future without the threat of my father hanging over our heads. His taking Malachi and Wolf and Rylan has only heightened that fear. If I have this baby... If we don't remove my father before it happens...

He could take the baby, too.

I shudder. "I don't have a convenient answer for you, Malachi. I wish I did. I'm not ready to end this pregnancy, no matter how complicated my feelings are about it. It's our only chance."

"I don't give a fuck about the plan," he says quietly. "Do you want it?"

That's the question, isn't it? I pushed back when Grace offered me the same option Malachi is right now, claiming I couldn't make that decision without the men being involved. In hindsight, it feels like an excuse. Not a single one of them would hold making that call against me. I have no doubts about that. "Since Azazel did his magic, I haven't felt so drained and exhausted."

"Mina, that's not an answer."

I know, but I don't *have* an answer right now. I sigh. "I do want it, I think. I haven't really had time to process, and I—" Right here, right now, I can tell him the truth. The awful feeling in my throat gets worse. "I'm afraid to want it. Wanting something is a good excuse for the world to take it away. To have *my father* take it away." I press my hand to Malachi's broad chest. "I dared to want you and look what happened. You spent a week being tortured by him."

"It's fine."

"It's *not* fine." I suck in a harsh breath. "I won't ask you to talk about it if you don't want to, but I'm here if you do." They've listened to my story, but they haven't shared a single thing that happened to them in the time they were captive. I don't have a right to ask them to share if they're not ready, but the big black hole of information makes me uneasy. It's like we're walking on eggshells with each other.

I want to reclaim the easy feeling we'd just reached before my father ruined everything, but I'm not even sure how we accomplished it to begin with. When it comes right down to it, we've only known each other a short time. Things have been uncomfortable and filled with animosity more than they haven't. I shouldn't dare crave something I barely got a taste of in the first place.

Malachi frames my face with his big hands. "It wasn't as bad as you're imagining. I suspect he meant to soften us up, so he focused on isolating us and drugged us with something that made the starvation kick in quicker." His expression is so grave, it makes my chest hurt. "I couldn't think properly, but I worried about you. That was the worst of it, little dhampir."

This time.

If we don't do something about my father, it will be worse next time. He might try to forcibly breed them. The thought makes me shudder. "We have to kill him. We can't wait any longer."

"We can wait to start making proper plans until morning." He shifts his hands to my shoulders and gives me a squeeze. "Just let us take care of you tonight."

"You're the one who's suffered. I should be taking care of *you*."

He smiles a little. "This is how you take care of me." Malachi strips me easily, his big hands gentle on my body. It's not sexual, but it feels like a small eternity since I've touched him. I won't make assumptions. Not with us feeling so raw right now. But I'm only me, and I would have to pass through death's gate in order to not want this man. Maybe I'd even want him in the afterlife.

I don't know how this happened. A few months ago, I didn't even know he existed. Now, he's a cornerstone in my life and I can't imagine going on without him. The strength of that feeling should scare me—and it does—but it's like it can't find purchase in our reality.

I don't know if I believe in destiny, but I can't deny that Malachi and I feel destined.

We step beneath the spray and he pulls me into his arms. It feels so damn good to have his naked body pressed against me. Yes, there's sexual desire, but just touching him reassures a part of me that couldn't quite believe he's here and safe.

A horrible sound wrenches itself from my chest. Malachi hugs me tighter. "I'm here. You're safe."

I bury my face in his chest and sob until it feels like my body will shatter into a million pieces and crumble away to dust. It *hurts*, but at least I know I'm still alive. That he's still alive. We are here together, which is more than I could say twenty-four hours ago. It's like all my fear and rage have crystallized into the tears I shed in that moment. It's a purging.

I don't mean to kiss him. Truly, I don't. One moment, I'm sobbing and the next my mouth is on his and I'm climbing his body to wrap my legs around his waist. Malachi barely hesitates.

He kisses me back like he needs my air to breathe. One step and my back hits the tiled wall. He pins me there so effortlessly, it makes me shake with need. *Yes, this. This is what I need. Please don't stop.*

He breaks our kiss long enough to say in a strained voice, "I can't. Mina, you have to stop kissing me right now if you don't want—"

"Take me." I nip his throat. "I need you. Don't make me wait."

He growls something low in a language I don't recognize and then his big cock presses to my entrance. I'm wet but nowhere near where I need to be for him to plunge into me. It's *work.* He grips my hips and uses short strokes to fight his way into my body. It's not entirely comfortable, but I don't care. I need this as much as he does. More, even.

By the time he sheaths himself to the hilt, we're both shaking and panting. Malachi presses his forehead to mine. "You feel good, little dhampir. You feel like home."

"Bite me," I gasp.

"No." A slight shake of his head. "Not until we know for sure that it's safe." Malachi kisses me, stifling any protest, quick and rough. "I don't need my bite to make you feel good."

It's nothing more than the truth. He cups my ass and moves me up and down his cock, adjusting the angle until he hits all the right spots inside me and my clit rubs against him with every stroke. Immediately, pleasure coils through me. Need sparks low in my stomach, building and building. I missed this. I missed *him.*

"Getting started without us, I see."

He turns with me still in his arms as the curtain is wrenched back to reveal Wolf and Rylan. Malachi raises his brows. "Shower's not big enough for four."

"You look clean enough." Wolf eyes me hungrily. "Take it to the bedroom."

Rylan hands over a towel. "We'll be along shortly."

I give a strained laugh and press my forehead to Malachi's chest. "Sounds like a plan." It means an aborted orgasm right now but more pleasure in the near future. More, it means reconnecting. Maybe after we all get back in bed together, where this connection truly began, we'll be able to banish the strange distance that's cropped up between us since we reunited.

Malachi sets me down long enough to wash me quickly, ignoring my half-hearted protests that I can do it myself. It doesn't take long before we've switched places with Rylan and Wolf. I'm only half dried off when Malachi hauls me back into the bedroom and goes down on his back, me astride him. He plants big hands on my hips and looks at me like I'm his world.

A few weeks ago, I would have doubted this, would have wasted time looking for a trap. Surely no one can fall as hard and fast as we have for each other. I've fallen for the others, too, but with Malachi, it was strangely seamless after our first few initial bumps. I don't understand why he's so sure of me. Or why that feeling is so mutual. I should doubt. I should...

There's no room for should in this world. I almost lost him. I won't waste another moment doubting what we have when proof that it's there is so readily available. I don't know what the future will bring, but we have this now and I won't waste it.

I reach between us and grip his big cock, giving him a stroke and then lifting my hips to notch him at my entrance. It's easier to take him this time. I work myself down his length in a slow, glorious stroke. "You always feel so good."

"I love you, Mina."

My heart lurches and then steadies. Is this the first time he's said it to me? It feels like it. I hold perfectly still, letting the words settle through me. I never thought to find this connection at all, let alone with three men. But it's here, and I won't meet his bravery with cowardice.

I lick my lips. "I...I love you, too."

9

WOLF BOUNDS INTO THE BEDROOM IN A LEAP THAT takes him from the doorway onto the bed. The impact sends Malachi's cock even deeper inside me and I can't hold back a moan. Wolf grins. "I missed that sound."

"I missed you," I admit. "All of you."

Rylan joins us on the bed. It's only a king, so there's not a ton of room, but we make it work. He kneels behind me and presses his chest to my back. I close my eyes and soak up the skin-to-skin contact. It feels so good, I could almost be satisfied with stopping here, if not for the steady pulse of desire through my body.

"No biting," Malachi says firmly. "Not until we navigate the new limits."

I tense. "You think my blood's poison like in the dreams." Again, there's no reason for that to sting. If it is, it's some magical quirk and not a reflection of how much they want me, but I can't help taking it personally. Foolish in the extreme, but I'm too emotionally raw to hold back the hurt in my voice.

Rylan shifts my hair off my shoulder and kisses my neck in the exact spot he bit it in the dream. "You're pregnant, Mina. That means you need the blood more than we do. If we drain too much, we could harm you and the pregnancy. Best not to test it while we're...distracted."

Distracted with fucking me.

I try for a smile. "I suppose that's a fair argument."

"So glad you think so." I can hear the smile in his voice.

Wolf appears in front of me with a knife in his hand. "That only goes one way, though."

"Wolf," Malachi warns.

He grins, completely unrepentant. "That little monster growing inside her is half vampire. You can't honestly tell me that a little blood is going to harm it." He jerks a chin at me. "Besides, she looks like shit and she's lost weight."

I blink. "Wow, tell me how you really feel."

"You're even paler than me, love. A little blood will get you back into tip-top shape." He slices a long line across his forearm.

I don't hesitate. I lunge forward and grab his arm, hauling it to my mouth. The first taste is like...I don't have words. I've drank from all three of them before, and their magic is readily apparent in their blood. It was enough to boost my own power and even heal a recent injury. I wouldn't say it's old hat at this point but drinking from them hasn't surprised me since that first taste from each, unique in their own way.

This is different.

The flavor of Wolf's blood explodes against my tongue, sending a wave of pure need through me. I start moving on Malachi's cock, but I keep Wolf's arm in an iron grip. "More," I growl against his skin.

"Malachi?" Later, it will irritate me that Wolf looks to Malachi for guidance instead of taking me at my word. Right now, I can't think past the delicious taste of him coating my tongue and throat.

"Don't stop." His grip pulses on my hips, guiding me to the rhythm that feels the best, long slow strokes that have me rubbing him exactly where I need him. Rylan shifts behind me to run his hand down my stomach and press his fingers to my clit. Another long pull of Wolf's blood and I lose it.

I slam down on Malachi's cock, sobbing my way through an orgasm. It's good. Too damn good. But I don't want it to stop. "More!"

"Mina—"

"More. *Please.*"

Wolf gently pulls his arm from my grasp and then Rylan's is there, blood already streaming. In the back of my mind, a voice whispers that I should stop, that they need their blood more than I do, but I can't. It's like the first taste has peeled away my civilized layers, leaving only the animal beneath. I need their blood, their bodies. I need more.

Malachi moves me over his cock, his expression intense as he watches my face. It's not pleasure alone lurking in his dark eyes. I'm too far gone to nuance it out. Not with Rylan's blood like fire on my tongue. I moan and whimper, drinking deep even as another orgasm bears down on me. It's almost too much, but when has that stopped us?

My orgasm drags Malachi along with me this time. He growls my name as he comes, grinding up into me in the most delicious way. Rylan starts to take his arm back, but I dig my nails in. "Not yet."

"Mina." Malachi sits up and wrenches my mouth from Rylan's arm. I whimper and lunge for it, but he catches me lightly by the throat. His dark brows draw together. "Something's wrong."

"The only thing that's wrong is that you won't let me drink." My gaze snags on the throbbing pulse point in his throat. "Just a little more, Malachi. Please." I hate how wheedling my tone goes, but it's like I don't have control of my body, my tongue. "I'm *famished*."

He glances over my shoulder, conveying something to Rylan. It's *him* who lifts me off Malachi and makes a cage of his arms when I start to struggle. "Peace, Mina."

"Let me go."

"You're not acting like yourself."

I part my lips to command him to let me go, but Wolf is there, pressing his hand to my mouth. There's the tiniest cut there, barely enough to bleed at all and already healing supernaturally fast. But it's enough. It cuts my command off in its tracks.

Concern lines his handsome face. "This won't hold her long."

"Rylan?" Malachi is up and off the bed, moving around behind us. Part of me wants to twist to watch him, but I'm too busy licking Wolf's palm, trying to get every bit of blood I can manage.

Rylan's arms tense around me. "Either her seraph powers are lashing out after the separation...or it's the pregnancy. We have no way of knowing for sure."

"Why not just let her drink her fill?" Wolf switches hands, a new cut on his other palm that he presses to my lips. I moan a little in response and lean forward as far as I can with Rylan restraining me. "She's not going to be able to drain all three of us, and even if she did, she wouldn't kill us."

"Maybe," Rylan says darkly. "Or maybe she'd be glutted and keep going until there was nothing left. It could develop into frenzy."

Wolf laughs, but it's a shadow of his usual mad cackle. "You're thinking demons and werewolves, Rylan. Vampires don't frenzy."

I tense, waiting for Rylan to argue, but he just huffs out a breath. "There's always a first time. I've never seen a pregnant seraph, either. Who knows what happens during that time? They kept their secrets too close. We have no way of anticipating what happens next."

Malachi reappears in front of us. He's tied back his hair and has a knife in his hand. "We can't keep her restrained and gagged. We see this through. It's the only way to know for sure."

"Mal—"

He sends Rylan a sharp look. "We see this through," he repeats.

Something about this should bother me, but I can't think past the fact that Wolf's hand has healed and I've licked it clean. "More."

"Come here, little dhampir. I've got more for you." Malachi leans back against the headboard and motions with his free hand. "Release her."

Part of me expects Rylan to keep arguing, but he curses. "If this doesn't work—"

"Stop thinking so hard and go by instinct." Wolf shifts to kneel next to Malachi. His pale blue eyes take us in, more serious than he's ever been. "Worst case, she takes too much, we wrestle her off him, gag her, and toss her in a basement until we figure things out."

"That is not a plan," Rylan snaps.

"It's more of a plan than *you* have."

Malachi drags the knife down the line of his throat. Too deep. Blood pours down his wide chest to his stomach. Too much blood.

I want it all. My mouth waters. "Let me go."

Rylan releases me with another muffled curse. I waste no time straddling Malachi and licking my way up his chest to seal my mouth against the cut. Pure bliss has me closing my eyes and moaning. He wraps careful arms around me. "Take as much as you need. Everything I have is yours."

I drink in deep pulls. Even through my bliss, I can feel the tension rising in the room with each minute that ticks by. Wolf shifts next to us, fidgeting as if he went to reach for me and stopped himself before he could make contact.

Slowly, oh so slowly, the overwhelming need eases. The cut on Malachi's throat heals, and I give him one last long lick and press my forehead to his shoulder. For the first time since Wolf offered me his arm, my thoughts feel clear. My energy level, though, has plummeted. I can barely keep my eyes open. "I'm sorry," I whisper.

"There she is," Wolf says. He sounds relieved. "Had us worried for a minute, love."

"I'm sorry," I repeat. I can't look at them. I just acted like a monster. I wasn't thinking about them as men and people I care deeply about. The only thing that mattered to me was drinking as much of their blood as I could. "I don't know what that was."

Rylan abruptly stands. "I'm going to make some calls."

Malachi goes still beneath me. I don't have to lift my head to know they're sharing one of those speaking glances that contain entire conversations. His and Rylan's history lends to that sort of thing. They've certainly known each other long enough. A shudder works through Malachi's body. "You're sure?"

"We don't know enough."

"She'll make demands."

"She always does. We'll have to deal with her eventually. Might as well get something out of it in the process."

I don't hear him leave, but the bond I share with each of them tugs as Rylan moves away. Maybe one day I'll be able to pinpoint their location exactly, but for now I just get the vague feeling of increasing distance as he moves away from the house. I sigh. I can't keep burrowing into Malachi's chest like a coward. This—whatever this new complication is—needs to be faced.

"You're not a coward," Malachi says softly.

"Nah, not a coward." The bed shifts as Wolf tosses himself down onto it. "Just a cute little dhampir-slash-seraph in over her head."

I forgot—again—that they can read my mind now. Or at least glean my thoughts and feelings on occasion. Before they were taken, one of the things Malachi and I were working on was teaching me how to shield properly. Another thing to add to the list.

I take a deep breath and straighten. My current exhaustion level feels different than I've gotten used to. It's less feeling sick and unable to function than feeling deliciously sated. That will scare me later, maybe. I press my hand to my stomach. For once, the awful nausea that usually rises after I eat is nowhere in evidence. "The little monster *would* prefer blood to solid food." I can't live on blood, though. At least I'm reasonably sure I can't. All the dhampirs I know lean human in that way.

But then, I'm not human at all, am I?

"Do seraphim eat?"

"I have no idea." Wolf props himself up on one arm next to Malachi. "Rylan will come back with answers."

I twist to glance out the door he left through. He's farther afield now, and he seems to be pacing. "Who's he going to contact?" Silence greets me and I turn to find them looking at each other as if deciding how much to tell me. Irritation flashes. "I would think we're past you hiding things from me."

"It's for your own good."

I glare at Malachi. "I think it's better *I* decide what's for my own good. I'm not a child. Stop treating me like one." When they still hesitate, frustration blooms. "If we manage to kill my father, *I* will take his place. How long do you think I'll be able to hold his throne when you don't treat me like an equal?"

He smooths my hair back, expression intense. "Don't ask us not to take care of you, little dhampir. It's too much to demand."

"You're being unreasonable. I'm not saying don't take care of me. I'm just asking for you to stop keeping information from me. What harm can information do?" The question isn't fair, because information can do a good deal of harm and we all know it. But I am *not* a child.

Still, he relents and drops his hands. "He's contacting his mother."

10

AFTER DROPPING THAT BOMB OF AN INFORMATION piece, Malachi refuses to answer further questions, stating that it's Rylan's business and if he wants me to know, he'll tell me. We end up in the shower again to wash off the blood, but we keep it brief. Later, when I'm tucked safely between Wolf and Malachi, silently tracking Rylan's continued pacing with my mind, I allow myself to think about what Malachi did and didn't say.

I thought these three were the last of their bloodlines. In hindsight, that seems very naive. Malachi, yes. It's known that he's the last one. *Everyone* knows it. But while my father might have extensive information on the seven bloodlines, it's not information he ever shared with me.

Rylan still has family alive.

I open my eyes to find Wolf watching me. Malachi's body

is loose and relaxed at my back. Impossible to tell whether he's actually asleep or if he's merely giving us a measure of assumed privacy. I swallow hard. "Do you have family alive, too?"

"Sure." He shrugs as much as someone can while lying on their side. "There's a few cousins. My parents and sister are no doubt still rampaging through Europe and leaving chaos in their wake."

He says it so casually, too casually. Wolf talks about his family the same way I recited what my father did to my knee to keep me from running. No one keeps their words totally emotionless unless they're hiding something ugly beneath.

Sadness swamps me, even as I tell myself I'm being silly. Surely I wasn't expecting any of these men to have the idealistic childhood of which I was deprived? I know better. My father might be a monster, but there's something to be said about power corrupting. Immortals don't manage to stay alive for hundreds of years by being nice and kind. Doing so is as much as inviting enemies to come in and cut off their heads.

I shiver. "You're not close."

"No." Another of those shrugs. "My parents were even more unhinged than I am. It didn't make for a restful childhood. I haven't seen them since I left a very long time ago. It's better for everyone that we don't congregate often." He won't quite meet my gaze. "I take great pains to ensure I don't cross paths with my sister more than strictly necessary."

I can relate, though it makes me sad. I reach up and cup his angular jaw. "I'm sorry."

"You keep apologizing for things that aren't your fault." His grin is quick and sharp. "Careful, love. Someone might see that big heart of yours and try to take advantage."

"I don't have a big heart." Sometimes I think I don't have a heart at all. All my life, I've never known peace. First, because I was raised in my father's compound as a powerless dhampir, which translated to a useless dhampir. Then, when I was sent to Malachi as a sacrifice, all I could focus on was gaining my freedom. But even that wasn't enough because my father's been hunting us ever since we broke the blood ward around his old house. Every step of the way, I've been looking out for myself first.

Maybe if I hadn't been, Wolf and the others wouldn't have been taken.

"Get that look off your face." He presses his thumb to the spot between my brows. "You could use a little less worrying. Malachi and Rylan are both too brilliant not to figure this out."

The right words but the wrong tone. I frown. "There's something else you're not telling me."

"Wolf." His name is barely more than a rumble from Malachi. A warning.

I sit up. "We *just* had this conversation. Why are you still keeping things from me?"

"I—"

Wolf stretches out and props his head on his arms. "What he's trying to figure out how to bend over backward to avoid saying is that there's a distinct possibility that Rylan's mother will take the questions about seraphim as an excuse to hunt you down and kill you."

I flinch. Judging from what everyone has told me about

seraphim, I can't exactly blame her for wanting me gone, but...
"I'm getting heartily tired of having a target painted on my chest."

"Get used to it, love. Those who remember what your people did when they held power will either want to use you or kill you."

The walls feel like they're closing in. I hadn't thought beyond removing my father as a threat. He's been larger than life for so long, it never occurred to me that there would be others baying for my blood if they got half a chance. I shudder. "It will never end, will it? We'll be running forever."

"Eh." Wolf shrugs, totally relaxed. "We just need to kill your father, convert all his little followers to being *your* followers, and you'll be set. Our enemies come after you, we'll kill them. They send others, and we'll kill them, too. Eventually, they'll realize we're too powerful to fuck with and don't have any intention of repeating history and they'll leave us alone." He grins. "Except for the odd assassination attempt to keep us on our toes."

"You are not making me feel better." My voice comes out reedy. I press the heels of my hands to my eyes. "I thought it would be over after we kill my father."

Malachi wraps his hands around my wrists and gently tugs them down. "When you have eternity, you'll come to appreciate the little things that break up the monotony."

It speaks volumes that they consider *assassination attempts* to be little things. "I could use a little monotony in my life."

He gives my wrists a gentle squeeze. "You'll have it." He glances at Wolf and shrugs. "Besides, if it ever gets to be too much, we can always jump to a realm that's never heard of seraphim. That would create other challenges, but it's always an option."

I lick my lips. I don't know that I'm ready to abandon *this* realm, but the escape hatch option calms me all the same. "Are there many other realms? More than this one and Azazel's?"

"No one's ever tracked them properly, but there are at least dozens."

Wolf laughs, sounding more like himself. "No one's tracked them properly because they've died trying." He flicks Malachi's hair off his shoulder. "Might be a fun challenge in a couple hundred years when the baby bats are grown and have flown the nest."

I blink. "Did you just call the…" I'm not quite able to call it a baby yet. It's *not* a baby. It's a cluster of cells. "Did you just call it a *baby bat?*"

"It's as good a name as anything."

A reluctant smile pulls at the edges of my lips. "You can't even turn into a bat."

"Rylan can." Wolf makes a show of shuddering. "Freakish thing. Too big. Could probably carry you on its back if you wanted."

I feel the man in question approaching. "I think he's done with his call."

"Spooky."

I shoot a look at Wolf, though I can feel Malachi watching me. There's a tension about him that makes me think he'll lunge forward if I suddenly topple. It's a strange thought, that he'll always be there to catch me. I trust him. I do. But my need to stand on my own is nearly overpowering. "I'm fine, Malachi."

"You're shaking."

I hate that he's right. I lift my hand and study the tremors as Rylan closes the distance between us. He's moving inhumanly fast, and I shouldn't be able to track him so effectively as a result. The seraph bond is freakish.

Too much change. Too much information. Too little time.

Dealing with the long-term effects of the seraph bond will have to wait until we're out of crisis mode, whenever that happens. *If* it ever happens. The thought depresses me. Instead of responding to Malachi's question that isn't a question, I twist to face the door as Rylan walks through.

His expression is a careful mask, giving away nothing. "I spoke with her." He doesn't make us wait, thankfully. He just sighs. "It's...complicated."

"Threat?" This from Malachi. He links his fingers through mine, tense enough that I can tell he wants to haul me back into his arms and wrap me up in himself. I'm not entirely opposed to the idea, but I just got done telling him that I need to stand on my own, so I can't walk back on it now.

Rylan shrugs. "She didn't start making threats, but that's not how she operates. At this point, she'll wait and see, and if she decides she needs to act, we'll hear from her in a decade or so. She *did* give some interesting information."

He moves, strangely stilted, and sinks onto the edge of the bed near me. "When seraphim became pregnant, they would retreat into their fortified locations for the duration. Based on when they'd go missing, it was estimated that the gestation cycle is similar to a vampire or human. Forty weeks, give or take." He looks at me, dark eyes conflicted. "We don't have information on what happens during that time. They would disappear with a retinue of vampire...servants...and reappear with a brand-new seraph baby. Most of the time, the vampires that went with them were never seen again."

Wolf whistles. "Suppose it's too much to pretend they were just moved to different colonies."

"They wouldn't be able to because of the seraph bond."

Damn it. I press my lips together, fighting against the urge to scream that it's not fair. That we deserve to catch a break *for once.* "You think they drain the vampires and kill them during the pregnancy."

"We don't know what to think," Malachi cuts in with a warning glance at the other two. "Seraphim don't drink blood."

"Other ways to drain a victim."

"For fuck's sake, Wolf. Shut up."

Drain them of power, of life, of what makes them *them.* The thought leaves me cold. I was only interested in blood when I lost control earlier, but that's the thing: I wasn't in control at all. If that hunger had switched to more magical things, I wouldn't have been able to stop it. Neither would the men. "You have to leave."

"Absolutely not."

I glare at them all. It's not easy with them arranged the way they are, but I make a valiant effort. "I am not endangering you just because I'm pregnant. That wasn't part of the bargain."

"None of this was." Rylan shrugs. "We work with the realities we have. It might be that you're just mirroring a full vampire more than your seraph half. They need to consume large amounts of blood."

"I've never needed blood before." I was never even offered it until Malachi, so if that was a requirement of living, I would be long gone. "That doesn't make sense."

"It makes as much sense as anything." He doesn't look away. "We are working on theory here. There's no reason to jump to the worst-case scenario."

"That's enough." Malachi's voice has gone harsh. "We all need sleep and then we need to come up with a plan for tomorrow. Everything else can wait."

Until I get hungry again. Or the magic goes weird. Or...

We have been more unlucky than we've had breaks that went in our favor. First we used me to break the blood bond that trapped Malachi, only to discover I was actually half seraph and had bonded with all three men. A seraph bond isn't something that can be reversed.

Then, we finally thought we'd have some time to figure things out, to explore the new powers the bond had allowed us to share, only to have my father show up and take the men.

Then, I find out I'm pregnant, the one way most likely to dethrone my father, only for the pregnancy to be just as freakish as I am. The kind of freak who endangers those I've come to care most about.

It's only as I'm falling asleep that a small voice in the back of my mind points out I didn't immediately throw up the blood I consumed.

That I feel better.

11

I WAKE UP WITH RYLAN AT MY BACK AND WOLF NUZ-
zling my breasts. It's a low, dreamlike adjustment from sleep to
awareness, and I shift against them, enjoying the feel of their
naked skin sliding against mine. They're here, with me. It's not a
dream. They're safe...at least for now.

Rylan cups my hip. "Awake?"

"Yes," I whisper.

Wolf chuckles against my skin. "Good." He moves down, drag-
ging his mouth over my stomach. He nudges Rylan's hand to my
thigh, and Rylan responds by gripping me there and lifting my leg
up and out, opening the way for Wolf. They move seamlessly the
way they always seem to. Even when they're arguing, there's always
this awareness between my men. It speaks to their long history.
Everything about their relationships speaks to their long history.

Malachi isn't in bed with us. I can feel him faintly in the distance, some miles away. He doesn't seem distressed, but... "Malachi?"

"A little morning hunting." Wolf playfully nips one thigh and then the other. "Don't worry about him."

Rylan sighs against my temple. "You can't just tell people not to worry."

"You're right." Wolf laughs, high and unhinged. "I have a better way." Then his mouth is on my pussy.

He kisses me thoroughly, tasting every inch with long swipes of his tongue. He ignores my clit almost entirely, a delightfully aggravating experience as he tastes me. "Missed this," he murmurs against me. I missed it too. I don't get a chance to say it much, though, because he chooses that moment to thrust his tongue into me, making my back bow and drawing a cry from my lips.

Rylan slides his other arm between me and the mattress, hugging me to his body as Wolf ravishes me with his mouth. I can't think, can't move, can only whimper and shake. "I need—"

Wolf sucks hard on my clit, but he stops before I can reach my peak. I cry out in protest, and his laugh goes dark. "Feels good, doesn't she?"

It takes my pleasure-drugged brain a few moments to realize he's not talking to me. He's talking to Rylan, who's gone tense behind me. His arms provide a loving cage that keeps me immobile. He's so still, he might as well have been carved from stone. "Wolf," he snarls.

"Smells good, too." Wolf inhales. He licks a line down my thigh. "Smells *tempting*."

"We shouldn't."

Understanding crashes over me. I know what they're talking about now. Malachi might have instructed them not to bite me, but they want to. *I* want them to. "Do it," I whisper. "Please."

"As the lady commands."

"*Wolf!*"

But it's too late. He snaps forward, quick as a snake, and bites my thigh. I come instantly, crying out so loudly that it's almost a scream. Wolf takes one pull and then another, each one like a pleasurable tug on my clit that only spikes my orgasm higher.

He stops. A little spark of power flares on my thigh where he's cut his tongue to speed my heeling, and then he climbs up my body. He brushes a quick kiss to my lips, too quickly. I'm not his final destination, after all. Wolf shifts just a little so he can take Rylan's mouth.

Rylan moans and his grip on me goes almost painfully tight, claws suddenly pricking my skin as he starts to lose control. They move, pressing close as if they can get to each other through me. It might be enough to make me feel immaterial, but this is what I want just as much as I want them to focus on me. I love that my men love each other. I wouldn't have it any other way.

Wolf lifts his head. "You need it more than we do. Take what she's offering before you lose control and hurt her." His voice goes hard. "Because if your stubbornness causes her harm again, I *will* kill you."

"Wolf, no." My protest is faint. "Don't force him."

"Everyone is so fucking selfless. So damn ready to bend over backward to be polite even though it weakens you." He curses.

"You're too damn shortsighted. One bite, Rylan. You're not going to lose control now, but the same can't be said if you wait too long."

Now it's Rylan's turn to curse. "You're right."

"I know."

Still, he doesn't bite me. I think we're all remembering back at the safe house where Rylan lost control after denying both of us for too long. He bit me too deep. I don't think he would have killed me, even if Malachi and Wolf hadn't intervened, but the memory is too fresh to argue with.

I tilt my head to the side, offering my neck. "I trust you."

"Gods." He speaks low and soft, but the words are lost on me as his teeth sink into my skin. Wolf presses us onto our backs and then his big cock is at my entrance, pushing steadily into me. The first pull from Rylan's mouth has my orgasm rising again, and Wolf working his cock into me only heightens my pleasure.

I want it to be like this always.

Rylan only takes four pulls, but it's more than enough. It's like it incites something within the three of us. A flame. A desperation to be closer, to make our pleasure last longer. A desire for *more*.

He wrestles Wolf and I off him. Wolf lands on his back with me astride him, his cock still buried deep. He thrusts up, laughing in a choked kind of way. "Better hurry, Rylan. Missed this too much to last long."

I plant my hands on his chest and start to ride him. "Yes, Rylan. Hurry." I'm going to come again. It's as if all the misery and suffering from the last week have held back a wave of pleasure so strong, it threatens to sweep me away entirely. I'm not sure I mind. The harsh reality will return all too soon. I want this while we have this chance.

"You can last. Both of you," Rylan bites out. His weight disappears from behind me for a moment and I hear him rustling through the nightstand drawer. He snorts. "The demon *would* ensure we're fully stocked on lube."

"Azazel has his priorities in order." Wolf hooks the back of my neck and tows me close to claim my mouth. Kissing him is rarely soft and never what I expect. This time is no different. His tongue is fierce against mine, filled with things left unsaid. I meet him stroke for stroke, never stopping riding him even as I'm sighing and gasping against his lips.

The mattress dips as Rylan returns to us. I already know what to expect. What comes next. We've done this before. If we live through the coming confrontation, we'll do this many times again. The thought makes me shiver. Rylan palms my ass, that delicious tremor in his hands. "You up for this?"

I break Wolf's kiss to snarl, "Fuck me, Rylan. Don't hold back."

"You heard her." Wolf laughs and then he reclaims my mouth with teeth and tongue.

Rylan doesn't ask again. He spreads lube over me and works his fingers into me in slow strokes. It hasn't been that long since we've done this, but he's nothing if not thorough. When I first met him, I thought he was an unbelievable ass. I still think that sometimes, but beneath his cold exterior is a man who cares far more than anyone would guess.

Anyone except Malachi. And Wolf. And now me.

He presses his cock to my ass. He hasn't always been careful with me in the past—I haven't always *wanted* him to be careful with me in the past—but he's being careful now. Neither he nor Wolf are small men, and the sensation of fullness is almost too much as he seats himself within me entirely. Rylan kisses the back of my neck. "Good?"

"Yes." I can't move, impaled as I am between them, but I still try. "Please. More."

"Love it when you say please," Wolf mutters against my temple. "Rylan?"

"Yeah." Rylan plants his hands on my hips and starts to thrust slowly into me. I squirm and moan, but in my current position, all I can really do is take what they give me. I kiss Wolf's throat, setting my teeth against his skin there. I have no fangs to pierce, but I suddenly want to.

I bite him anyways. Just to do it. His cock jerks inside me and he hisses. "Need something, love?"

"Yes." I stroke his throat with my fingers. A blink and the tips tingle, transforming to claws. Rylan is still fucking me slowly, but I can feel how his attention is now focused on my hand. If I try to rip out Wolf's throat, he'll stop me. I hope. I lick my lips. "Can I, Wolf?"

He tilts his head back as much as he can in our current positions. "Drink your fill, love."

Malachi is on his way back. I can feel the distance closing between us, him racing in our direction in a blur too fast for the human eye to follow. When he returns, he'll make us stop. He laid down very reasonable guidelines fewer than twelve hours ago. Reasonable guidelines that we're flaunting right now.

I can practically feel Wolf's pulse on my tongue, a steady beat begging me to taste. I don't want to wait, and I don't want to play things safe and slow. "Just a little taste." I'm lying and we all know it.

"Put the claws away, Mina." Rylan releases one hip and leans down to cover my hand with his own. "Let me."

I don't want to. I want to draw Wolf's blood, to take it into my body the same way I'm taking his cock right now, to make it my own. What Rylan's saying is smart, though. I don't want to hurt Wolf. I just want to taste him on my tongue. "Yes."

Rylan's skin tingles against mine. I don't know if I've ever felt him use his magic like this before, but it's pleasant. As my fingers shift back to their normal shape, his grow sharp and claw-like. He drags three down the center of Wolf's throat. Not gouging him, but deep enough that it will take some time to heal.

Wolf digs his hands into my hair and guides my mouth to his throat. I hardly need any encouragement. Everything about this feels good, feels *right*. Rylan picks up his pace a little as I drink from Wolf. With how we're arranged, he's essentially fucking both of us. Wolf's grip on my hair spasms and he moans a bit with each pull I take from his throat.

Pleasure builds inside me in slow waves. We're not rushing. It feels like we're spinning a web of desire around each other, each slide of their cocks, each swipe of my tongue against Wolf's throat, the delicious friction of all their skin against all of mine... It all increases the sensation of something magical taking place.

Rylan curses. "Too fucking good. I'm going to—" His teeth sink into my shoulder.

Just like that, I'm coming. I sob against Wolf's throat, writhing through an orgasm that curls my toes. Rylan pulls out at the last moment and a bare second later, his seed lashes my ass and lower back. He barely gets out of the way before Wolf rolls us. His hand is at the nape of my neck again, urging me back to his throat. "More, love. Bite me again."

"Wolf—"

"*Fuck off.*"

Something's wrong, but I'm too far gone to understand what. I wrap my legs around Wolf's hips and urge him deeper as I follow his command. The wounds are almost closed. I won't get as much as I want. *I want...* With the barest thought, my teeth grow sharp in my mouth. They nick my lips, but I don't care. I have what I need now.

I bite him.

He groans, low and deep, driving into me as he comes. Hot blood scours my tongue and I barely have the presence of mind to stop biting him and drink. Each pull makes him drive into me harder, which only makes my orgasm crest again. We're caught in a loop. It's too good to stop.

The door crashes open hard enough to bounce off the wall. The boom startles us enough that we freeze. Malachi stalks into the bedroom, his expression forbidding as he takes in the scene in front of him. I have the presence of mind to remove my mouth from Wolf's throat, but there's no covering up the mess. We're both sticky with his blood and other things. Even the sheets are soaked. "Mal—"

He starts unbuttoning his shirt. "You took too much."

Shame heats my skin. "I didn't mean to." I brush my fingers over Wolf's high cheekbones. His eyes flutter a little, but he looks almost drugged. "What's going on? I've taken more than this before and he didn't act like this."

"Felt too good," Wolf murmurs. "Couldn't stop coming."

It sounds startlingly familiar. It's how *I* feel when they bite me. Pleasure so strong that it overtakes all else. Orgasms that rise and rise and rise until the bite ends. But that doesn't make sense.

I crawl out from under him as Malachi sits on the bed and hauls Wolf up to sprawl across his wide chest. I gingerly touch my mouth. My teeth feel normal, my cut lips already healed. "I don't have a bite like a bloodline vampire. Do bites even work on other vampires? This is impossible."

"When will you admit it, Mina?" Rylan's tone isn't unkind as he sinks onto the bed next to me and wraps a surprisingly comforting arm around my shoulders. "You're not a vampire. You're a seraph. The rules don't apply to you."

12

I DON'T KNOW WHY IT STILL STINGS TO BE REMINDED that I'm not human, vampire, or dhampir. I'm something else, something rare and dangerous and unknown. "I'm aware."

Rylan sighs. "I didn't mean it like that."

"It's fine."

"It's not." He tugs me closer as Malachi offers a forearm to Wolf. Wolf bites quickly and drinks deep. Within a few minutes, he's looking more like himself again. Relief makes me a little woozy. We've exchanged blood before—all of us. It's never been truly dangerous, not like it appears to be now.

No. That's not true. From the moment I met Malachi and then the others, they've been dangerous to me. One bite taken too far could end my life. It's something none of us have really spoken at great lengths about, but we've all been aware of it. This is different.

I've never been dangerous to them.

When Wolf finally sits back, Malachi levels a look at me. "We'll talk about this later. Right now, we need to discuss our next step with Cornelius."

I start to argue that we need to talk about it now, but his rationale makes sense. If we don't survive the fight with my father, it won't matter that I'm dangerous to them, because we'll all be captive or dead. What a cheerful thought.

Rylan huffs out a breath. "Why don't we start with where we are? Did you figure out the state or the town, at least?"

"Still Montana. Best I can tell, it's the next town over from the compound."

"Azazel didn't take us far." Wolf shakes his head, a grin pulling at his lips. "That wily bastard."

Malachi nods. "We won't fly under the radar for long. We have to move while Cornelius is still scrambling to search for us."

Every time he says my father's name, I have to fight back a flinch. He's no demon to be summoned by speaking his name, but I can't shake the strangely superstitious feeling that we shouldn't say it. I swallow past my fear. "Even if I kill him publicly, what's to stop my siblings from finishing what he started? They've all had their powers for years at this point. I won't win in an endless string of duels." Our plan had seemed so reasonable—if a long shot—when we put it together on the run after escaping Malachi's house. My time with Grace poking holes in it has only made me doubt myself. My father is *powerful*. He stopped Rylan, who is a bloodline vampire who can change his entire form, with a single word.

Seraph or no, my father can compel me to do whatever the hell he wants if he gets a chance to speak.

"It has to be public. Witnesses. You have to take control of the entire compound with one shot by killing him and doing it bloody enough that they won't challenge you. He's already primed them to fall in line when faced with a strong leader. We just have to convince them that *you're* that strong leader."

I give Malachi the look that statement deserves. Most of my siblings considered me beneath their notice while I was growing up, and I preferred it that way—fewer people who wanted to kick me when I was down. That might have benefited me growing up, but it hardly primed them to follow me as a leader. "The only chance we have is an attack he doesn't see coming. He needs to be dead before he's able to use his magic. If he gets one word out, we lose. How are we supposed to manage that in public?" Otherwise, we're delivering ourselves right into his hands.

"I don't know yet."

I can't stop my bitter laugh. "Isn't that rather crucial to the plan?" It's not fair to take my frustration out on Malachi. He didn't exactly choose to be held captive by my father for over a hundred years or to be bonded to a seraph when the attempt to gain freedom came with more strings than any of us expected. He needs my father dead just as much as I do.

"Earplugs?"

I'm already shaking my head at Rylan's suggestion. "A few years ago, one of his subordinates tried it. His magic might not work well over electronics or long distances, but normal means of muffling sound don't seem to have an effect." Logically, they *should*, but magic likes to play by its own rules.

"It was worth a suggestion." Rylan gives my shoulders a squeeze. "We'll figure it out."

"We keep saying that, but no brilliant ideas have come." I'm not being fair and I know it, but I can't stop. I shrug out from under Rylan's arm. "I'm going to wash the blood off." I hold up a hand when all three of them tense. "Alone. I need to think."

It's only when I step beneath the water nearly hot enough to scald that my brain starts working properly. I close my eyes and let the worries and mental knots unwind. The men are here. That's already a huge victory and one that shouldn't have been possible if my father had his way. He'll have paraded them before the compound the way he always did in the past with his conquests. Losing them is a blow. Being the one to steal them away *is* a power play that will help establish me as a leader if I manage to kill him.

What they're asking for feels impossible, but they don't have the same history with him that I do. No matter how hard I fight it, my father remains larger than life in my mind. The same isn't true for my men. I need to stop letting my fear control me and *listen.*

By the time I finish my shower, I feel halfway human again. I smile a little at the irony. I might feel halfway human, but I'm not human at all. There has to be some way I can use that. If the seraphim were so feared as a whole, there has to be a reason why. Surely it's not just because when they have sex with vampires, they can bond with them. There must be more.

There has to be.

The men aren't in the bedroom, which is just as well. We

ruined another bed. I stare at the bloodstains and grimace. Someday, when this is all over and we've settled somewhere, we're going to have to invest in plastic sheets on the bed we have sex in and have a strict no-biting rule in the bed we sleep in. I shake my head and pull on a dress from the closet. Like the fridge, it was fully stocked when I arrived. Once dressed, I follow the faint tug of the bond downstairs to the kitchen.

They all look up as I descend the stairs, their expressions varying degrees of wary. Malachi is the one who approaches me. He's always the one who takes that first step, and I'll love him forever because of it.

I clear my throat. "I'm sorry. I shouldn't have snapped. I'm scared, but that's no excuse. You're trying to help."

Malachi takes my hand and tugs me down the last stair and into his arms. "It's nothing. A few sharp words are hardly enough to require forgiveness."

"Still."

He chuckles. "You're forgiven, little dhampir." After one last squeeze, he sets me back. "Shall we feed you?"

Instantly, my mouth waters at the thought of more blood, but he turns to the fridge and that feeling sours. I shake my head. "No. I'm good. I'm not hungry." In fact, I feel the opposite of hungry. I want to fling myself away from the fridge and what it contains.

Malachi frowns. "When did you last eat?"

I start to say this morning, but that's not true. No matter how good it felt to drink Wolf's blood—and Malachi's last night—it doesn't change the fact that it's not *eating*. I touch my stomach. "I'm not hungry," I repeat. When all three of their attentions sharpen on me, I sigh. "I ate... Um." I can't remember. I haven't eaten since the demon deal, I don't think. Maybe the morning after? I vaguely remember being sick. "A day or two."

"Malachi." Rylan says into the silence after my answer. "This isn't outside the realm of possibility. We discussed this. We don't eat. The...baby...is half ours."

"Mina is not a vampire." Malachi speaks softly but he might as well have yelled. "She is not going to be harmed by this pregnancy."

Irritation flares. "For the last goddamned time, *I am standing right here.*" I march past him. "I feel fine, so we're going to chalk this up to some combination of pregnancy, magic, and my strange bloodlines. We have bigger things to focus on. If, at the end of this, we're all left standing, then you can worry and pester me about the pregnancy. First, we need to deal with my father."

Rylan looks like he wants to argue, and I can't see Malachi from my current position but I can feel his displeasure like a flame at my back. Wolf, of course, seems as relaxed as ever. He grins, flashing fangs. "I take it your shower helped."

I nod. "My father has to be our priority. The rest of it can wait. I don't know how we're going to get onto the compound, let alone take him out, but you're right. It's our only option, and we need to do it quickly." I clear my throat and sink down onto the chair next to Wolf. "I'm not going to pretend I have a brilliant plan, but I'm done running." I place the map of the compound I drew for Grace on the center of the table.

It feels strange and a little uncomfortable to sit like this, all of us around the table, but better the table between us so no magic goes funky and we end up having sex for the next three days. I would *love* to be able to do that, but the longer we wait, the higher the chance my father finds us. I don't think there's anything magical about this house. Its location being out of the way and entirely unconnected to any of the vampires is enough to keep us off the radar for a few days, but it won't last forever.

We have to move now. The sooner the better. The vampires disappearing will have disconcerted my father and he'll be desperate to reclaim them. It's likely not enough to make him sloppy, but it's better than nothing.

At least we're not reacting this time. He is. That has to count for something. We have to *make* it count for something.

I quickly update them on the information that Grace passed on. From Grace's information, it seems like not much has changed since I left, aside from increased patrols, and why would it? My father doesn't see me as a threat. He's not going to alter his world because I might be gunning for him.

It's a mistake I hope we can exploit.

"I would wager none of the soldiers he has on-site are powerful enough to be more than a slight inconvenience for you." I point to a spot just south of the main gate. "This is where Grace spent most of her time scouting the place. Because the compound is tucked into a canyon, there are vantage points here, here, and here." I touch each place with a finger.

Malachi takes the pen from me and marks them with a small X. "That will help."

"If you say so." The idea of storming the base with the men is *world's* different from storming the base with just Grace. We should be able to get all the way to the heart of the compound without anyone stopping us.

But that's where it stops being easy.

I stare at the drawing, searching it for anything I've missed. It's as detailed as I can remember, with a few edits from Grace. "The biggest issue is my father's power."

"Yeah. About that." Wolf's pale blue gaze goes contemplative. "He has to speak to use it, right?"

"Yes. He can glamour and the like without speaking, I think. But to use his commands, he has to speak them." I turn to him. "But how do you keep him from speaking?"

Rylan drums his fingers on the table. "Injury would be the easiest way. It won't stick long, not with how old and powerful he is, but even he would take a few seconds to heal a crushed larynx. Maybe up to a minute if someone tears out his throat."

I know my father is powerful, of course. I was raised under his thumb, and I've seen what he does to those less powerful than him. In that compound, *everyone* is less powerful than he is. Still, it feels particularly worrisome to have *these* vampires admit he's a formidable foe. It's not new information, but it still sends a shiver down my spine. "We still have to get close to him to do either of those things."

"Maybe." Malachi sits back, his chair groaning beneath him. "When's the last time you did a ranged attack, Wolf?"

Wolf shrugs, but it's nowhere near the careless body language he normally has. Tension bleeds from him through the bond, winding tighter and tighter. "I haven't had reason to. I'm out of practice."

Malachi hesitates, glances at me, and then sighs. "We should call in your sister." He holds up a hand when Wolf tenses. "I know it's not an ideal situation, but you can't diagnose issues with your blood the way she can. And she's a better ranged attacker than you are by a long shot."

"My sister *poisons* blood." Something almost fearful edges into Wolf's voice. "You're out of your damn mind, Mal. She's as likely to kill Mina as she is to help with anything. There's a reason I haven't seen her in fifty years." He glances at me. "You think I'm a loose cannon? My sister is worse."

He said something to the same effect last night. I'd felt something akin to pity then, but now I don't know what to think. I look between them, taking in their very serious expressions. "It seems like a long shot with greater risk than rewards."

"Mal's right," Rylan says reluctantly. "Lizzie could shoot Cornelius from a mile away and he'd never see the attack coming. It would give us the opportunity to take him out while he can't speak. He's still going to be able to fight, but at least he won't be able to compel."

Wolf's distress flares so brightly, I reach over and cover his hand with mine. He's shaking, just a little, fine tremors that send a surge of fierce protectiveness through me. I look at the other two men. "We're not doing it if Wolf isn't okay with it. It's easy for you to say things will work out and this won't backfire, but it's his family." His family that makes this mad vampire look well-adjusted. I don't know what to think of that. All I know is that I don't want any of my men harmed.

What are the chances of all of us making it out alive?

I don't have an answer for that question.

No one at the table does.

13

IN THE END, THE TRUTH IS WE HAVE NO OPTIONS. Unless we nullify my father's ability to compel, any plan we make is dead in the water. Even dropping a bomb on the compound—if any of us were willing to do it—wouldn't guarantee my father's death. He's too old, too savvy. He'd find a way to survive even that, and then we'd have mass casualties on our heads.

My life was a living hell in that compound, and my father wasn't the only one responsible for that. But not everyone was a monster. Not everyone chose cruelty when they could offer kindness instead. I won't say those who showed me kindness as a child were the majority, but they existed. Even if they hadn't, I'm not willing to sanction the murder of every adult and child in the compound. It's too high a cost.

So Wolf phones his sister, Lizzie.

He makes the call in the other room, but even I can hear his side of the conversation, so no doubt Rylan and Malachi can hear both sides. Sure enough, they exchange a long glance. Malachi sighs. "Lizzie is going to be a problem, but we won't let her hurt you."

"Maybe you can fuck her, too, and then the seraph bond will take care of that."

I stare at Rylan. Of all the things to suggest... "Please tell me you're joking."

"Mostly." He grimaces. "It *would* simplify matters, but we'd have to make sure Lizzie didn't kill you during the bonding process, and that's more difficult than you can imagine. She's too unpredictable."

There it is again.

The evidence that they have such a deep history that extends many of my lifetimes in the past. Malachi was in that house for a hundred years, but before that, he was friends and lovers with Rylan and Wolf and others. Maybe even Lizzie. I'm not sure how I feel about that. Not jealous, exactly. Just...strange.

"If you want to know, you can ask."

I jump, startled out of my thoughts by Malachi's low voice. There's no mistaking what question he's talking about. I force myself to meet his gaze. "Were you lovers? Either of you?"

"Not me." Rylan doesn't exactly shudder, but it's there in his voice. "I prefer my throat intact."

"I was, briefly." Malachi holds my gaze. "Does that bother you?"

"I don't know," I say honestly. "I don't think so, but it feels strange. We've been very isolated up to this point, so part of it is that, I think." I'm going to have to get used to the feeling that there are great swathes of these men's history unavailable to me, at least outside sharing stories. We have the future, and that's enough. It has to be. "I guess we'll deal with it as it comes."

Wolf walks back into the room, unhappiness in every line of his body. "She's in LA right now, but she's all too happy to dive into the chaos and do a little murder." His voice goes up on the last part of the sentence, obviously mimicking his sister. "She'll be here in about ten hours."

Every hour is a risk at this point, but this delay is one we can't avoid.

Wolf comes back to the table, but instead of reclaiming his chair, he sinks down onto the floor next to me. He puts his head in my lap and wraps his arms around my waist. I freeze. "Wolf?"

"I'm fine."

He's lying. Now that he's touching me, the bond flares between us, soaked in his misery. I tentatively clasp the back of his neck and massage a little. He responds by going boneless, though his unhappiness doesn't abate. I look at the other two men. "Someone explain this to me. Now, please."

Rylan shifts. "Fifty years ago, Lizzie set Wolf on fire."

"*Excuse me?*"

I know him well enough to recognize that his cold tone is a way of masking his emotions. He holds my gaze and continues. "They had a disagreement and she felt that was a reasonable way to deal with it. He almost died."

The table creaks beneath Malachi's hands. "You didn't see fit to mention that *before* we called her."

I get a sense of Rylan's internal conflict through the bond, but none of it shows in his face or tone. "We don't have any other options."

I keep massaging Wolf's neck and try to think past the fury that burns through me. "Tell her not to come. There has to be another way."

"No other way." Wolf speaks against my thigh. "She's the best. If she helps, it's a sure thing—at least that part of it."

Killing my father is the top priority, but I never expected the cost to be so high. That feels very naive right now, with Wolf feeling so small and human against me. I want to protect him, to wrap him up and keep him safe, and that isn't the world we live in. "It's not worth the cost."

He tightens his hold around my hips. "I'm fine," he repeats.

He most assuredly is *not* fine. Not when he's clutching me like his favorite toy. I look to Malachi and Rylan for help, but they're staring at each other and engaging in one of those silent arguments that I'm not a part of. Malachi is obviously furious they didn't tell him what happened, and Rylan is clearly digging in his heels on his stance.

Huh. Apparently I can read them a lot better now, whether from the experience of being in close proximity for a few weeks or maybe as a side effect of the bond. Their argument ultimately won't change anything. I have to go off what Wolf says. He's my priority right now.

"Feels nice."

I blink. "What?"

He shifts enough to look up at me out of one eye. "Being the priority. Wish it were better circumstances."

Guilt slaps me hard enough to make me shake. "I'm sorry. I know I said it before, but things haven't calmed down enough to talk about it. I'm sorry I compelled you." Bad enough to do it, but then to simply not talk about it as if it's beneath notice? I can't believe I let it get this far. "Maybe now isn't the time to talk about it…"

"Mina."

The shock of him saying my name makes me tense. "Yes?"

"You're strong."

It's such a random statement that I stare down at him blankly. "What?"

"Don't apologize for being strong."

I feel like we're having two different conversations. "I'm not apologizing for being strong. I'm apologizing for forcing you to do something you didn't want to do. Strong or not, it's not right. I love you." The last comes out in a rush. "I love all of you. I don't want to hurt you and I don't want to take your choices away. I shouldn't have compelled you. You *are* a priority to me."

"Seems like a silly thing to apologize for."

"Why would you say that?"

He straightens and wedges himself between my thighs. Wolf isn't as tall as Rylan and Malachi, but he's more than a few inches taller than me. We're nearly the same height like this. He holds my gaze, his blue eyes strikingly serious. "If you hadn't made that call and forced the issue, we'd still be in your father's tender care.

Call me unhinged all you want, but I'm not a fool. I underestimated you." He gives a sharp grin that almost looks like the old Wolf. "Maybe I should be the one apologizing."

"I *compelled* you." Like my father does to those around him. I took away Wolf's willpower and forced an answer out of him.

"Yep." He laughs suddenly. "Gods, love, but seeing you twist yourself up over this is enough to make me feel loads better." He leans up and presses a kiss to my lips. "If you need my forgiveness, you have it."

I sigh. "That doesn't help with your sister."

"Just sleep with her, too, and it will be a moot point."

I frown. "Why is everyone so invested in me adding people to the bond? That's the opposite of what we need if she's as bad as you say." Not to mention three bed partners is *a lot*. I can't imagine trying to juggle the needs of more, let alone one as volatile as Wolf's sister seems to be. No matter what else is true of our little group, the caring between us is real. The men's goes back several human lifetimes. Mine is newer but no less valid. "Besides, even if I could compel her, it only works in spurts. It's not something that I can hold to ensure good behavior."

"I'm joking, love." Wolf shakes his head. "No matter what else is true, I do *not* want to be linked that closely with her. Better to get her agreement to pull this off for us and then to go our separate ways."

I don't have answers. I don't know that I ever have. But we have time and I want to wash away that faintly lost look in Wolf's eyes. *This* I know how to do. *This* is a way I can help. I cup his face between my hands and kiss him. I start gently, teasing his mouth open and delving inside. For once, Wolf doesn't immediately take control. He meets my kiss halfway, but he allows me to lead us.

He tastes so purely *Wolf* that I moan a little. I nip his bottom lip. "Trade places with me."

He moves all at once, surging up and lifting me into his arms. I expect him to do as I say, but instead he whisks us into the living room. I end up on my knees between his thighs, staring up at him. "Wolf?"

"Floor's killer on the knees."

The small act of caring only drives the desire to return the favor all the more. I slide my hands up his thighs. "I'm taking off your pants now."

"Don't let me stop you." But he's the one who undoes the front of his pants and lifts his hips so I can work them down his thighs. It takes a little maneuvering to get them fully off, but it's more than worth it when I reclaim my position with nothing between me and Wolf's body. He's so deceptively beautiful. The aura and mohawk kind of shield that truth, but when I have him like this, there's no denying it.

I can hear Malachi and Rylan still speaking softly in the kitchen. Arguing softly, more like it. I can't do much about that right now. They'll argue and debate and eventually come to an agreement on how to deal with Lizzie and the coming confrontation. I've given them the map of the compound and I'll provide any additional information they need, though we all are aware that it's somewhat outdated, even with Grace surveying the compound from a distance. I can't do anything to help the plan right now.

But Wolf?

I can help Wolf.

I want my vampire back. I don't like the brittle look that's appeared in his eyes. Of the three, he's always seemed the most untouchable, the one who is carefree and more than a little wild. Right now, he seems almost...human.

"Wolf." I lean down and rub my cheek on his bare thigh. "Do you know what I would like right now?"

He sifts his fingers through my hair. Not tugging. Not guiding. Just touching me as if the very contact soothes him. "What?"

"I want to take care of you." He tenses against me so I press a kiss to his thigh. "Will you let me do that?"

"I thought you were going to tell me to fuck your mouth." He gives a low, strained laugh. "Quite the twist there, love."

"Is it so shocking?" They've taken care of me since we met. Yes, there was some circling on whether they wanted to keep or kill me—at least where Wolf and Rylan were concerned—but ultimately that threat didn't last long past the initial meeting. They have bolstered me, have encircled me, have lifted me up to make me stronger.

The very least I can do is return the favor.

More, I *want* to.

Wolf shakes his head slowly. "No. Guess it's not." He smiles slowly, almost looking like himself again. "Very well. Do your worst."

"Oh, Wolf. I'm not going to do my worst." I wrap my hand around his thick cock. "I'm going to do my very best."

14

OF THE THREE MEN, I LOVE SUCKING WOLF'S COCK THE most. He's the only one who is more than happy to finish in my mouth if I'm so inclined. Both Rylan and Malachi were always so focused on not missing an opportunity to impregnate me. I might start like this, with their hard length pressing against my tongue, but it never lasted long before they'd lose patience and haul me up their bodies to fuck me.

Wolf alone let me take my time.

I suck him down, keeping my gaze on his face. He watches me closely, gaze almost predatory. I shiver and take him deeper. The power balance here is a knife's edge between him and me. He could easily overpower me. I hold his pleasure and pain between my lips. I suck hard and am instantly rewarded when he hisses out a breath and lets his head fall back to rest against the couch.

It's not submission. Not truly. But he's letting me hold the reins for now.

The temptation to take him deep, again and again, until he loses control is almost too much to bear. That's not what I want right now, though. I want to make him forget all his worries, to release the stress tightening his shoulders, to get him to focus only on me.

I tighten my grip on his cock just a little and release him with my mouth. He starts to open his eyes, but I'm already moving, licking down his length to play my tongue along his balls. Wolf's thighs go tight on either side of me. "Fuck," he breathes.

I started this process for him, but I can't deny my pure joy at my slow exploration. It's not the first time I've done it, but it's the first time he's given me this much control. His legs are shaking and he's dug his fists so hard into the couch, he's punctured the cushions, but still he doesn't try to rush me.

I keep sucking and teasing, ignoring the ache that blooms in my jaw as a result. It doesn't matter. I can take more than a little discomfort, especially as Wolf's expression goes slack and languid. Finally, when time ceases to have meaning and we're both shaking with need, I move back the smallest bit.

"Wolf." I flick my tongue against the underside of the head of his cock. "How do you want to finish?"

His mouth works for several moments before words emerge. "Come up here, love. I want to be in that sweet pussy when I come."

I give him one last long suck, taking his entire length in, and then release him and climb up to straddle his hips. "Like this?"

"Yeah. Like that."

I sink slowly onto his cock. It feels good enough that I nearly lose myself, but this isn't about me. Not this time. It's about him and what he needs. I work myself up and down his length, rolling my hips in a way that makes crimson overtake the blue of his eyes. "Let go, Wolf." I cup his face with my hands. "I've got you."

He wraps his arms around me and pulls me closer yet. I can't move well like this, but it doesn't matter because he's taking over. He holds me tightly and pumps up into me. I moan. Gods, this feels too good. "Wolf, I—"

He bites me.

I come so hard, I see stars. I'm vaguely aware of him licking his way up my throat and taking my mouth as he follows me over the edge. Each near-violent thrust up into me makes my orgasm surge higher. I'm sobbing against his lips and he's holding me closer yet. Just when it edges into being too much, he slumps back to the couch, taking me with him. I lie there with my ear against his chest and I can *feel* his tension easing. I've never experienced anything quite like it. Is this what the men feel from me without my shields? It's not mind reading. Wolf's thoughts are his own. But I can almost see his emotions. It's strange but not bad. Not bad at all.

I kiss his throat. "Better?"

"Yeah." He huffs out a laugh. "Yeah, I guess it is." Wolf squeezes me. "Take care of me anytime you want, love."

I sense Rylan and Malachi coming closer. They certainly don't make any sound to give away their presence. I turn my head enough to see them standing in the doorway to the kitchen. Rylan looks conflicted but Malachi's face is an expressionless mask. "We have a plan."

Wolf gives me one last squeeze and helps me off him, though he doesn't let me get far. Instead, he pulls me back down onto his lap and wraps his arms around me. I tentatively send out a tendril of awareness through the bond, acting purely on instinct. He still feels calmer, but the inner turmoil beneath the calm surface is causing ripples. There's not much I can do about that, not until we see ourselves through this mess.

He closes me out gently, pushing me away as he reinstates his shield. It's not as impenetrable as a stone wall—I can still get a hint of what he's feeling beyond it—but he closes me out all the same.

"Sorry," I murmur. I didn't mean to invade his privacy. No, that's not accurate. I *did* reach out, but I still have hardly any idea of what I'm doing.

"I dropped my shields. It was practically an invitation." Though there's still a faint tremor in his tone, he sounds more like his old self.

Malachi and Rylan sink onto the couch across the coffee table from us. Malachi leans forward and sets my makeshift maps on the table. "We have a plan." He points to the two buildings near the rear of the compound. I've labeled them as armory and gym. "We'll set fire to both of these. We'll do it during the day so as to minimize casualties."

Rylan takes over. "It should draw most of the guards in that direction, both to put out the fire and to search for who started it. I don't think they're poorly trained enough to leave their posts completely abandoned, but it should alleviate some of the extra personnel." He pauses. "Then you come in through the front gate."

I blink. "That's bold."

"It's the weakest point. More, this conflict is as much about presentation as it is about killing your father. We need witnesses. The courtyard will have to be it." Malachi drags a hand through his long hair. He points to one of the Xs he made near the front. "We'll set up Lizzie here. Will she be able to see the courtyard from this location?"

I peer at the map, trying to hold it up to what Grace and I spoke of. I didn't leave the compound when I lived there, but I spent enough time staring at the surrounding area to know roughly what spot she had indicated. "It's a long shot."

"That's why we have Lizzie."

It seems impossible, but these three men have already proved themselves to be capable of impossible things. "I think so. We'd have to get him into the right position." I close my eyes and picture it. If she's aiming for his throat, he'd have to be facing the gates but at a slight angle leaning toward the shooter's position. "That adds to the impossibility factor, because getting him there will give him more of a chance to compel one or all of us."

Wolf tightens his grip around my waist. "Rylan has an idea, don't you?"

"Yeah." Rylan holds my gaze. "You're going in alone."

"*What?*"

"You're right. Your father's power is a threat while you get him into position. We can't guarantee he won't be able to use it, and if he does, we're more of a liability than a help." He nods at Malachi. "Mal will be setting fires. Wolf and I will go in to the east and west and do what damage to the forces we can. Maybe set a few fires ourselves if we can find a way to do it that won't result in more deaths." His dark eyes are sympathetic. "You were always going to be the one to kill Cornelius, Mina. It has to be you."

My chest threatens to close, but I haven't come this far to fold now. Which sounds great in theory, but the thought of having to face down my father alone makes me want to start running and never stop. I'm not so panicked that I don't notice the way all three of them tense up in response to my emotions. I have to breathe, to think, to process this. "Just...give me a second."

They sit silently as I battle through my instinctive denial. When we were initially talking about returning to that place and doing what was necessary to ensure our safety, at least I had the relative comfort of knowing my men would have my back. Walking through the front gates alone, even if the men won't be too far, feels like too much. I am stronger than I used to be, but I'm nowhere near as strong as my father.

He could kill me.

He'll certainly try.

I press my hand to my stomach. There's only one way to make him pause, and it means giving him information I'd do anything to ensure he doesn't have. It means trusting my men and the plan and myself in a way I don't know if I'm capable of.

Finally, I drag in a breath. "I don't know what will happen

to his compulsion if he's injured." All evidence suggests he needs to concentrate to use his powers, the same as the other bloodline vampires. If his concentration is broken, say by a blood bullet to his throat, the compulsion *should* break.

Am I willing to put myself under my father's control for even that long?

I open my eyes. I can't see Wolf, but Rylan and Malachi look at me solemnly. They know what they're asking, what we're risking. If I die, there's a decent chance it will hurt them, if not kill them. They're asking a lot, but they're putting so much faith in me that it staggers me. We'll only get one shot at this.

We'll either succeed or we'll die trying.

"I'm scared."

"I know." Malachi's eyes go soft. "We wouldn't ask if there was another way."

"I know." I run my fingers over Wolf's bare arm. Really, there's no point in letting panic win. This is the only way. If I think about it, it was only ever going to end like this, with me facing down my father once and for all. "You're both right. There is no other way. I'll do it."

Wolf finally sets me aside, though he laces his fingers through mine. "You'll have to take his head, and you have to do it showy enough to scare people into obeying you right off the bat. Lizzie will start the process, but that's the only way to guarantee that bastard doesn't come back to haunt us and no one challenges you while you're still reeling. Then we burn the body."

I wait for the idea of killing my father to inspire some hesitation or even guilt, but the only thing I feel is grim resolution. It's him or me. If I want a chance at the future, to give my...child...a future, then he needs to die.

Wolf could probably form his blood into a weapon to do it for him. Rylan could partially shift and tear my father's head from his shoulders. Malachi could burn him until there's nothing left to heal.

Theoretically, I'll be able to do all three with the way we seem to be able to borrow powers from each other. But my control has left something to be desired. I don't have the training and while sometimes they manifest, they never do it reliably. Whether the pregnancy was to blame or just my lack of experience is up for debate. I wasn't able to use them even before I found out I was pregnant.

I'll have to do it the old-fashioned way. "I'm going to need a blade," I finally say. "Thankfully, Grace left behind a whole stack to choose from."

"Mina." Malachi watches me closely. "If you don't want to do this—"

"There's no other way." I shake my head. "Let's not waste time trying to find other options. If this is the plan, we need to perfect it."

Malachi hesitates but finally nods. "Let's go over it step by step."

15

WHILE I'M NOT FEELING PARTICULARLY CONFIDENT, AT least I know the steps of the plan by heart after we go through it a few times. Whether or not it will work... I don't know. There are too many things beyond our control, which means too many things that could go wrong. The most important of these, of course, is Wolf's sister.

She should arrive any minute.

Rylan and Malachi went hunting earlier, returning rosy-cheeked and brimming with health. They fed Wolf, but no one offered to feed me. I can feel the hunger stirring—I'll have to eat again before we attack the compound—but I'm just grateful they've stopped trying to feed me human food. The very thought disgusts me. That revulsion will worry me later, when I have time and energy to think about the implications. First, I have to focus on the threat directly in front of me.

Lizzie.

I don't expect to feel her approach. It's been so long since I've been around other vampires, and I certainly didn't feel my father and his people break into the mountain home. This is different. Very different. I lift my head, turning in the direction of the sensation. It feels a bit like what I imagine all the water being sucked out before a tsunami hits feels like. "What is that?"

"Lizzie." Wolf bites out her name. "She's not bothering to shield. She wants us to know she's coming."

Without saying another word, we move into the living room. It's got a clear view of both front and back doors. Malachi nudges me to the love seat that backs a wall with no windows and then pushes Wolf gently down next to me. "Let me and Rylan do the talking."

"That won't work and you know it." Wolf's voice shakes a little, but he's more composed than he was this morning in the kitchen. "She won't be satisfied with that."

I place my hand on his thigh, a fierce protectiveness surging. If this vampire thinks she can come in here and harm those I care about, she'll have to go through me to do it. I squeeze his thigh. "She will not touch you." Something akin to power thrums through my voice. It feels strange, and all three of the men tense in response.

The door flies open before anyone has a chance to comment on it.

I don't know what I expected of Wolf's sister. Perhaps someone like him, who dresses in a style that's Victorian crossed with underground club scene. Someone who feels out of time. Someone fiercely beautiful and wildly unhinged.

The woman who walks through the door looks like a suburban housewife in her dark jeans, cream knit sweater, and knee-high boots. Her dark hair is pulled back into a perfect, sleek ponytail and her makeup is present but tasteful. She's wearing a *floral headband.* She's attractive in a generic kind of way, but she doesn't possess the kind of beauty that will stop people in their tracks. She's devastatingly normal.

At least until I look into her icy blue eyes. There's no warmth there, no soul.

She smiles, flashing fang. "Hello, baby brother."

Wolf goes still beside me. "Lizzie."

She surveys the room, her gaze flicking dismissively over Rylan before lingering on Malachi. "Interesting company you're keeping these days." Her grin never wavers. "Nice to see you out and about, Mal. Silly of you to fall into that trap in the first place."

"Lizzie," he rumbles. "You'd better be here to help rather than cause unnecessary trouble."

"I never cause trouble unnecessarily." She finally looks at me, blue eyes assessing. "So this is the new girlfriend. Welcome to the family, sweet girl." She takes one step toward me and laughs when all three men jolt. "Relax, lads. If I was going to kill her, I wouldn't have walked through the front door."

Rylan makes a vaguely snarling sound that shouldn't have been able to come from a human mouth. "Don't fuck with us, Lizzie."

"Can't blame a girl for having a little fun. Everyone is so *tense.*" She walks over to the chair where Malachi sits and props a hip against it. "Now, tell me who you want me to kill. I feel a tad bit guilty about the little fire incident last time we met, so I'm willing to play nice for the duration." She feathers her fingers through Malachi's long hair. "Besides, I couldn't resist the temptation to see old friends."

She's toying with Wolf. Maybe with me, too. Testing. I might even appreciate how thoroughly she disrupted the room with a few short sentences if the stakes weren't so damned high. "You're not going to be able to kill anyone. We simply need you to shoot him in the throat."

She turns those eerie eyes on me again. When I first met Wolf, his eyes spooked me. Compared to Lizzie, he seems downright welcoming and normal. It's strange to realize that. Wolf has become known and familiar to me in our time together, but I don't think that's a possibility with his sister.

She's fucking terrifying.

Lizzie stops playing with Malachi's hair and straightens. "Explain. My baby brother was sparse on the details."

I open my mouth, but Rylan beats me to the punch. It's just as well. For whatever reason, Lizzie seems less interested in messing with him than with anyone else in the room. He leans forward. "We're going to kill Cornelius Lancaster."

She doesn't seem shocked. She doesn't react at all. "Big game you're hunting. Even with my help, he's likely to kill you all." She laughs, a thread of madness in the sound. "I'm not getting close to that canny old bastard."

"We don't need or want you to get close." Rylan points to the maps on the coffee table. He and Malachi found topographical ones somewhere, so they've overlaid those with my drawings to get a better idea of exactly what we're working with. "You're the best long-range attacker in this realm."

"Flattery will get you everywhere." She scans the map and then looks back at him. "Explain what you want. Then I'll tell you my price."

"You'll be here." He points to the X south of the compound. "It's high enough that you'll have a clear shot of the court-yard." Rylan moves his finger to the X drawn in the compound. "Cornelius will be there. We need you to shoot him in the throat and put enough power behind it to destroy his vocal cords."

"He'll heal fast."

"That's our problem."

More likely, that's *my* problem, but I appreciate the sentiment. Even if I'm the one facing my father, we're all in this together. I lean a little harder against Wolf. He hasn't moved since Lizzie walked into the room, tracking her the way a mouse tracks a cat. It's disconcerting in the extreme.

Rylan sits back. "Will you do it?"

"Sure." She shrugs. "If Wolf comes home."

I'm already shaking my head. "No. That's out of the question."

"Be quiet, little girl. The grown-ups are talking." She turns to Rylan. "You swept him away after that little misunderstanding and it put me in a bad way with our mother. Wolf needs to come home."

"No," I say again. I start to stand, but Wolf clamps an arm around my waist and keeps me sitting. "No," I repeat. "Whatever price you need, *I'll* pay it. Anything else is out of the question."

She raises an eyebrow, looking unimpressed. "What could

you possibly offer me that's worth the risk I'm taking? You're a nobody. If you were someone, I would have heard of you by now."

I'm not about to tell this dangerous woman that I'm a seraph. But that's not the only bargaining chip I have. I catch Malachi's eye and he gives a tight nod. He'll follow my lead. Rylan and Wolf will follow his.

I gently disentangle myself from Wolf and stand. "I'm Cornelius's daughter. His heir."

She narrows her eyes. "You say that, and yet the fact remains that I haven't heard of you. You could be anyone playing dress-up." Her eyes flare crimson for a beat before returning to their normal icy blue. "You don't feel particularly powerful. Smells like bullshit from where I'm standing."

"If you're aware of that much about my father, then you're aware of the stipulations about what it takes to become his heir." A gamble, but she's right. I have little in the way of bargaining power. If we succeed, that will change, but first I need to convince her.

Her gaze flicks to my stomach and her eyes flare crimson again. Lizzie shrugs. "So you're pregnant. That doesn't mean your story holds up. His children would be smart enough to get declared heir before they started sharpening their knives and aiming for that bastard's back."

"I prefer a more direct route." I wave my hand at the three men. "My father has never seen power that he hasn't tried to claim for his own. There's a reason *this* is the stipulation to become his heir. If I try to do this the proper way, he'll lock me up, take the baby, and claim it as his own via one of his mistresses, and likely try to claim the father as well." No need to tell her that he almost accomplished that goal already.

She studies each of the men in turn, finally landing on Wolf. "Is my brother the father?"

It's tempting to lie, but I have a feeling she'll know if I do. I shrug. "I don't know who the father is at this point. We won't know until I have the baby, and that will only happen if we survive what comes next."

"Hmm." She taps a finger to her bottom lip, painted a perfect pale pink. "If you're lying to me, I'll take it poorly."

I think I hear Wolf inhale sharply behind me, but I don't look away from his sister. "I'm not lying."

"So it seems. Not telling the full truth, but not lying." She shrugs. "Ah well, if the little beast inside you is really Radu blood, then our mother will skin me alive if I don't help now. Let me see." She starts for me, and both Malachi and Rylan jump to their feet. Lizzie smirks. "*Relax*, lads. I'll just do a scan. Nothing sinister." She reaches out and presses her fingertip to the back of my hand. A faint tingle goes through my entire body in a wave and she raises her eyebrows. "Interesting."

"What?"

"You don't seem the type to consort with demons, but there's a faint..." She licks her lips, gaze distant. "Cute little shield. The embryo is fine. Powerful little bugger, but too early to know the flavor." She refocuses on me. "I'm in. I'll do what you ask."

I don't breathe a sigh of relief. This was only the first step, and I'm not naive enough to believe Lizzie until she actually shoots my father. "Your price?"

"If you're successful in this cute little coup, you'll owe the Radu family a favor." Her smile goes knife-sharp. "And you will entertain us for a few days in your new compound."

I don't need to look at my men to recognize the trap. If—when—we succeed, that will put me at the head of the Lancaster bloodline. For better or worse, I will be a power whose choices mean something, affect the balance of our world. I lift my chin. It would be smarter to negotiate the favor away and entertain them while promising nothing, but I won't do that to Wolf. He feels the same way about the rest of his family as he does about his sister. Having them in close proximity will be a hellish experience for him. I refuse to put him through it. "I will not be entertaining anyone in the foreseeable future, but I am willing to negotiate a favor, provided it does no harm to me, my men, or my people, either directly or indirectly." Still too wide an offer, but I need her and she knows it.

Her grin widens. "Very well. A favor it is." She turns back to the map. "Walk me through the nitty-gritty details."

I sink back onto the couch as Rylan and Malachi launch into a brief overview of what they need from Lizzie. Fine tremors work their way through my body, the adrenaline letdown nearly making me sick to my stomach. Though I can't hide my physical reaction to the confrontation, I refuse to give in to it entirely while Lizzie is in the room.

Wolf laces his fingers through mine. Through the bond, I feel a wave of gratitude from him. I'm sure Malachi and Rylan will have thoughts about my choice later, but I can only do what I think is right. Rylan seems to have a complicated relationship with his family, but there's no fear there. Malachi has no family left at all. Surely they wouldn't expect me to throw Wolf to the, well, to the wolves?

I squeeze Wolf's hand and listen as the other two men go through an abbreviated version of the plan. I note that they leave out a few key components. Smart. Really, we have no reason to trust Lizzie with all the details. The only thing she needs to know pertains to my father, the courtyard, and her long-distance attack.

She finally sits back and laughs a little. "This should be fun. When do we start?"

"At dawn."

16

AFTER WE GO OVER THE PLAN ONE LAST TIME, RYLAN escorts Lizzie off the property. I keep part of my attention on his presence, monitoring his emotions for any spike that might indicate she's attacked him. It's getting easier to keep track of the men. They all shield too well for me to get much more than a faint impression, but I think that's preferable for everyone. I don't want to invade their privacy, and I look forward to a time when I'm able to get my own shields in place.

If we survive the next twenty-four hours, maybe I'll even manage it.

"We will."

I glance at Malachi. "You know I hate it when you do that."

"It's difficult not to when you're thinking so loudly." He takes my hand and tugs me against his chest so he can wrap his arms around me. Wolf said he needs a little time alone and headed in the opposite direction of both his sister and the town. His presence along the bond doesn't feel as calm as Rylan's, but he's not in a full-out panic state anymore.

This is, I realize, the first time Malachi and I have been alone in quite some time. I run my hands up his chest and look into his dark eyes. "There are more ways tomorrow could go wrong than there are ways it could go right."

"I know." He cups my face and drags his thumb along my lower lip. "But we've survived impossible scenarios already. What's one more?"

"That logic is so incredibly flawed."

He gives a brief smile. "It's the only logic I have."

I don't understand how he can be so steady, so unafraid, so sure things will work out. "Even injured, my father is a significant threat. He's stronger than me, faster than me, and—"

"He's not more determined than you." Malachi holds my gaze. "He'll be fighting for his life. You'll be fighting for so much more." He presses a kiss to my forehead. "We won't leave you to do it alone. All three of us will be fighting our way to you. You just need to survive until we get there."

Survive and prove I'm strong enough to rule.

I tuck myself under his arm. "Lizzie asked a question earlier..."

I don't know if it's the bond or merely Malachi's intuitiveness that has him sensing the direction of my thoughts. "About the baby's father."

"Yes." It's something I didn't even *think* could be an issue, mostly because I've only been focusing on the immediate future and survival. But the fact remains that no matter what magic is capable of, science reigns supreme when it comes to eggs and sperm and the like. Which means that this baby has a single biological father. It's strange to think of it as a baby. I've barely come to terms with the fact that I'm pregnant, let alone what the end result will be.

Still, the last thing I want to do is cause harm if I can avoid it. I just don't know if I *can* avoid it. "I don't want anything to come between the four of us. It feels like every time we find some measure of peace, we get kicked in the teeth and something happens that messes everything up. I don't—" I take a deep breath. "I said I want to keep the pregnancy and I meant it, but I also don't want the baby to be a point of contention."

Malachi smiles gently. "Come, little dhampir. Do you really think so little of us that we'd fight over a baby like dogs with a bone?" He sifts his hands through my hair. "That baby is ours. All of ours. The genetics and powers matter little."

Some tension I didn't realize I was carrying leaks out of me. I press my forehead to his chest and let him hold me for a few beats. "I want this to work."

"I know. It will."

There's plenty for me to fear. I should focus on what happens tomorrow, for one. But I can't help spinning out a future with several children, with a *family* that's built on love and respect instead of fear and threats. I have a chance at that future with Malachi and Rylan and Wolf. We just have to survive long enough to take it.

"Okay." I lift my head. "Okay. Thank you."

"I love you." He says it softly, as if it's a simple truth and not one that rocks me every time those three little words leave his lips. "I love them, too. We are a unit, Mina. All four of us. I know this hasn't been an easy journey and it's not likely to get easier, but we *will* prevail." His hold on me tightens before he seems to force himself to relax. "We will cut down anyone who threatens our future. *Anyone.*"

With that kind of promise, what can I do but return it? I go up on my tiptoes and press a kiss to his lips. "Starting tomorrow, with my father."

I half expect a night that feels like our last night in this world, but everyone is sober and distracted. Malachi keeps his arms around me, but both Rylan and Wolf pass by with casual touching as we settle down for the night. They're all too wired to sleep, but I can feel it pulling at my eyelids, a tyrant lord demanding their due.

"You need to eat."

It takes me a moment to realize Malachi is talking to me. "I'm not hungry." It's not strictly true. My stomach is empty and craving blood, not food. But considering how Malachi's reacted to *that* fact so far, I don't think he'll welcome the news. Not to mention part of me is scared to feed that way again. What if I lose control? Our plan is too carefully balanced to have one of the men out of commission because I went too far and drained too much.

"Little dhampir." He shakes his head. "I might not understand what's going on, but that doesn't mean I'll allow you to go without."

"You can't harm us," Rylan says from where he's just pulled

on a pair of lounge pants. "We're stronger than you and there are more of us. If you get out of control, we're more than capable of handling it."

I blush. I can't help it. "I get overwhelmed."

"That's just practice, love. All baby vamps get a little wild." Wolf flashes fang. He's not quite back to normal—I don't think he will be until we're done dealing with his sister—but he's a bit more of his wild and charismatic self.

"Come, Mina." Malachi practically carries me to the bed and drops onto it with me in his lap. He holds me with my back to his chest and offers me his arm. "Drink."

"Are you sure?"

"Yes. I'll not have you weak simply because we don't understand what's going on. Obviously you're taking blood the same way a full vampire does. We'll not deprive you."

I press my fingers to my lips. "What if my teeth change again and I do damage?"

"Try to control it."

Considering I still don't know *what* is going on with me, trying to control it is a laughable objective. Still, for them, I will attempt it. "Okay."

"Your claws."

It takes a moment to realize he's speaking to me, to understand what he wants. I close my eyes and concentrate, trying to envision my fingers changing to claws the way they've done in the past. For a beat, nothing happens, but then a faint tingling starts at my fingertips. It's tempting to open my eyes, but I resist, focusing on that feeling, on expanding it until my nails shift.

When I finally look down, the tips of my fingers have morphed to dainty claws. They're small, but they're sharp. "Could I do more?"

"This is how training starts." Rylan leans forward to examine my new fingers. "You have to work up to a full shift, because if you panic halfway through..." He doesn't quite shudder, but the feeling is there in his voice. "It won't kill you, but it's a painful and scary experience. Better to wait until you master this first."

The thought of being stuck in some half-transformed state makes me feel vaguely ill. "I don't know if I'll ever be ready for that."

"You will." He says it with a quiet confidence that makes me take it as truth. Maybe someday I'll be able to shift into a giant wolf the same way he can and we'll run together. The thought pleases me. It's not something I would have sought out as an ultimate dream before now, but I want it. Another part of our future that I will fight to be able to experience.

I drag a single claw along Malachi's forearm. Not deep enough that it won't heal easily, but it also won't close immediately. He presses his forearm to my mouth and I drink greedily. The first explosion of his blood against my tongue feels so right that I moan. This. *This* is what I've been craving.

Drinking this time isn't the frenzy from before. I can feel that monster inside me, pressing up against my skin, but Malachi's blood sates it before it has a chance to crave more. Or maybe I just haven't depleted the energy I got from the last feeding. This is all so new, it's impossible to say for sure.

All I know is that I lean back a few minutes later, sated and sleepy. "Thank you."

"Sleep now." Malachi's words rumble through my back. "We'll look out for you."

I want to stay awake. I do. But with his blood thrumming through my veins, my body has other ideas. My blinks lengthen and deepen. I'm aware of Rylan reclining on the bed next to us and Wolf flopping on top of him with a casual intimacy that makes my lips curve.

Together.

We're together.

This is how I want it to be.

Always.

17

WHEN I WAS DRAGGED FROM MY FATHER'S COMPOUND and tossed in a car to be delivered to Malachi, I never thought to return. I wasn't supposed to live this long. I can admit that now, crouched precariously high in a tree and looking down over the familiar walls and buildings.

He planned for me to die by Malachi's hand. A convenient snack that got his powerless dhampir daughter out of his hair and kept the trapped bloodline vampire alive. Malachi and I were never supposed to get along, to fall in love. We were never supposed to join up with Wolf and Rylan and break the blood ward, awaken the powers no one thought I had, and come for my father's head.

It's happening now.

There's no going back.

"Can you make the shot, Lizzie?" Malachi's hand is warm where it's wrapped around my bicep. I'm not in danger of falling, but he's taking no risks. I don't move with the same supernatural grace as the vampires, but my balance is better than it's ever been. A good thing, that. I'm going to need every advantage I can come up with for the pending confrontation.

Lizzie is in the next tree over. She's wearing high-end workout leggings, a long-sleeved shirt, and a puffy vest. She's added a soft headband to her ponytail today. She looks like she should be jogging in some carefully curated park...except for the rifle slung across her back.

She narrows her eyes at the compound. "I can make the shot. This is well within my range."

I blink. I know this is why we risked asking for her assistance, but the compound has to be a mile away. Maybe more. "Even for your powers?"

She smirks. "Yes, little girl. Even for my powers. You get him where I can see him, and there won't be much left of his throat when the hit lands."

We estimated a timeline based on the worst-case scenario. Even so, getting my father out into the courtyard is going to be a risk. *He's going to compel me.* That's the one thing we haven't spoken about, that no one's addressed directly. To keep my father complacent enough for Lizzie's attack to land, I have to lose. There's no guarantee that his power will break when his concentration does, but I'm not one of his followers, happy to follow his instructions and open to compulsion. I will be fighting it every step of the way.

It will break.

It has to.

And that's when I'll strike.

"Then we move." Malachi scoops me into his arms before I have a chance to tense and drops down to the forest floor. Rylan and Wolf land soundlessly on either side of him. There's no need to speak. We went over the plan one last time before leaving the house. They'll deposit me just outside the sentry lines and I'll wait ten minutes while they circle around to their respective locations.

At that point, I walk into the compound to surrender myself and seek an audience with my father. Then the fires start. That should draw the extra soldiers away from the courtyard. My father will suspect the truth—that the three vampires are attacking—but he still views me as a powerless dhampir. He won't have reason to keep security around himself because he's never needed help to deal with me before.

I'll only have one chance.

The first faint hint of sunrise is fighting back the dark of the sky when Malachi sets me carefully on my feet. He hugs me tightly. "This isn't goodbye."

It might be. It's easier for things to go wrong with this plan than it is for them to go right. None of that matters now. We've come too far to turn back, which means this isn't the time or place for doubts. I pull him down for a quick kiss. "I'll see you soon."

He steps back and then Wolf is there, whisking me into a dip and planting a kiss on my lips. "Give them hell, love."

And then there's Rylan. He takes my hands and looks down

at them for a long moment. "Fear and pain can help motivate a change. Not panic, though. It's a fine line." He squeezes my hands. "You are *never* defenseless, Mina. Not with our powers flowing through your blood. Trust them and trust yourself." He kisses me quickly. "Stay alive."

There's a beat of hesitation, as if we're all waiting for someone to speak up, to call the whole thing off. The temptation is there—I won't pretend it isn't—but I stay silent and so do the men. One by one, they turn and melt into the trees. I track the growing distances between us for a few moments and then turn toward the compound.

I breathe the cold mountain air and allow myself to feel all the conflicting emotions being back in this place brings. Anger and sorrow and a strange sort of bittersweet nostalgia. Things were more bad than good while growing up under my father's tender care, but there were small spots of light in those first twenty-five years of my life.

My mother is a hazy, distant one. She died when I was still young, one of my father's many mistresses to be felled by the very purpose he had them in the compound to serve: birthing another dhampir. My father is obsessed with his progeny, with his bloodlines.

It's why he took my failure to manifest powers personally. That and the fact that I was determined to push back against his authority every chance I got. I smile a little, though it feels wrong on my face. We've been working toward this endgame since I was born. Now that it's time to act, my nerves ease and my path remains clear.

If I fail, I won't be the only one to pay the price.

I press my hand to my stomach. So much has happened in the last few days, there were moments when I actually forgot I was pregnant. It's far too soon to see physical changes, and with Azazel's temporary shield in place, most of the worst of the side effects have passed.

Should I get pregnant again, I'll have to figure out how to shield on my own. I shake my head and check my watch. I'll worry about the future tomorrow. Right now, I can't afford to be distracted. I take one last breath and start walking toward the compound.

I expect to be stopped. There aren't many sentries outside the walls, but only a fool wouldn't post at least a few people in the forest surrounding the compound. Vampire senses only stretch so far, after all, and an early warning system can mean the difference between life and death in a confrontation. My father is many things, but a fool isn't one of them.

He must really see me as less than a threat. It's the only explanation for why I'm able to walk up the dirt road to the compound gates. They're large enough to drive a truck through...and they're ajar.

"Quite the welcome," I murmur. The urge rises to turn and flee. If we meant to set a trap, my father certainly intends the same.

I lift my chin and push open the gate. Inside, it's exactly the same as I remember. Low square buildings, all in a uniform gray. Nearly indistinguishable from each other. Rationally, I know a year hasn't even passed, but it feels like several lifetimes since I last moved about in this place.

Since no one appears to stop me, I walk through the low buildings that serve as gatehouse and a place for the wall guards to rest between patrols, especially when the weather is intense. Both seem to be empty.

I see the smoke before I scent the burning: three large plumes stretching to the heavens. All three of my men have their shields locked up tight, so I only get the faintest impression of fighting as I step into the courtyard. I turn my focus from them. Now's not the time to be distracted. Not when I have my own part to play.

I stretch out my arms. "Where are you, Father? I've come to negotiate."

This all hinges on him coming to me. If he goes to fight one of the men first, we're in trouble. He could compel them to fight the rest of our group. It would hamstring the other two men because of their desire not to hurt the compelled person. It would ruin any chances I have of succeeding because I am no match for any of them. No, I *have* to make sure he comes to me instead.

I turn a slow circle, arms still outstretched. "I've come to take my place as your heir. You got your wish." I raise my voice. "I carry a bloodline baby. Will you honor your terms, or will you take the coward's way out?"

I feel him before I see him. He's circled around behind me, which is exactly where I want him now that I'm facing the front gates. I turn slowly as he walks out from between two buildings. For such a monstrous man, my father looks nearly as normal as Lizzie does. Silvering brown hair, vaguely attractive features that would be forgettable if not for the charisma he exudes wherever he goes. He weaponizes it now. It presses against me with a force that nearly sends me to my knees, getting stronger with each step he takes in my direction.

He smiles benignly. "Come now, Mina. You must know that you can never be heir. My people will never follow you."

"Let me worry about that," I grit out. He's not even compelling me, but it's hard to speak. Each breath burns as his magic seems to seek a way inside. I hate that feeling, like each inhale gives him a little more power over me, like even now, he's worming his way into my brain. "Will you keep your word?"

He shakes his head and tsks. "How am I to even know you're my child? You have no bloodline powers to speak of. You look exactly like your mother. Who's to say she didn't betray me with some other man to beget you? None of *my* children are such a constant disappointment."

How can his words still sting after everything he's done? I drop my arms. "So you'll break your word."

My father moves closer. His expression remains benevolent, but his words only get uglier as he lowers his voice. "I don't know what game you're playing at, you little bitch, but it won't work. Losing the three bloodline vampires was a temporary setback, and now you've returned them to me. If you truly *are* pregnant, then I'll happily cut that baby out of you the moment it can survive on its own." His smile drops. "You, of course, will not survive the process."

Over my dead body.

I glare. "You're making a mistake. Name me as heir—"

"*Kneel*, slut." His power slams into me, forcing me to my knees. "I don't know how you managed to find *three* of them, but I commend you on being so willing to open your legs to fulfill my aims. I suppose we'll find which is the father once the child is born." He leans down a little, more power infusing his voice. "Are you actually pregnant? Be honest."

"Yes," I bite out. I couldn't have lied if I wanted to. I *hate* this feeling. Like I'm a puppet to his whim. I'm screaming inside my head, but no sound leaves my lips except what he wills. It doesn't matter that he's done this to me before; it's not something I'll *ever* get used to.

If our plan succeeds, I'll never have to experience it again.

"The fires. Your men are responsible?" I clench my jaw and he drops the charming act, his brows drawing down. *"Answer me."*

"Yes."

"What is their plan?"

I was still a teenager when I learned the trick to dealing with his ability to use glamour to wrest answers from unwilling mouths. With most people, he seems to make them want to tell the truth so that they surrender their knowledge willingly, to please him. With me, he's always used brute force. It hurts, but there is some room to maneuver, depending on how vague his questions. "Start fires."

He stares down at me as if he wants to rip my head from my shoulders. "What is their plan? *Be specific.*"

I fight against the push of his power. To do anything else is out of the question. I don't know what Lizzie is waiting for, but I will buy as much time as I need to. I taste blood and grin up at my father. "To start fires," I repeat.

He clenches his hands into fists and releases them slowly.

"And after they start fires?" He bites out each word like he wants to rip into me with more than power.

"Fight."

"I swear to the gods, I will kill you now, child or no, if you don't stop being so damned difficult." When I don't answer, he throws up his hands. "Well?"

"That wasn't a proper question." A little bit of blood leaks from the corner of my mouth. I'm not sure where it comes from when he does this. There's no cut or obvious injury, but I always bleed when I fight him.

I sit back on my heels and look up. A wave of dizziness passes over me, but when it clears, I nearly sob with relief. A little red dot appears on his throat. "Father?"

"*What?*"

"I hope this hurts." My hand goes to my boot, to the long knife in the sheath there, both courtesy of Grace's bag.

"I changed my mind. You die—"

His throat explodes.

18

I SURGE TO MY FEET BEFORE THE BLOOD MIST HAS A chance to fall. My father is old. He'll heal far too quickly to hesitate now. It's why we couldn't risk a shot to the head. If he's still able to speak, he'll put a stop to any attack before I have a chance to finish it.

His power still lingers in the air, but it no longer feels like it's chaining me in place. I lunge at him, taking him to the ground even as he tries to stop the bleeding. His mouth moves, but no words come out. How many seconds do I have? Thirty? Twenty? *Ten?*

Fear gives me strength as I hack at him with the knife. One strike hits his hands, another, and then they're finally out of the way. It takes one glance at his throat to drive home how little time I have. It's knitting together before my very eyes. "No!" I bring the blade over my head and thrust it down, intending to impale his neck. It will be impossible for him to heal if there's a knife in the way.

I don't make it.

He catches the blade in the palms of his hands, the blade sliding clean through and catching on the hilt. Shock freezes me for a single heartbeat, and then it's too late. He wrenches the knife away. The momentum sends it spinning away from us. I follow the trajectory as horror rises with the realization that it lands too far away. If I go for it, he'll be healed by the time I get back to him.

Rylan's voice rises from the back of my mind, memory, or something else.

Never defenseless. Never weaponless.

Do not panic.

I scream as my father strikes up at me. Instinct has me lifting my hands to keep him from hitting my face. In my fear, I almost don't notice the tingling that spread from my fingers down through my hands. I shove back at my father and blink down as blood sprays where I make contact.

My hands are...transformed. It's not like before. There are no dainty claws that are sharp but ultimately less than useful in a fight. No, my claws look like Rylan's when he's a wolf. They're huge and wickedly curved and achingly sharp.

My father's eyes go wide. *No,* he mouths.

"*Yes.*"

This time, when I attack, it doesn't matter that he's trying to fight me with his bare hands. A blow from me, and there are no more hands to speak of. Another swipe and his throat is gone entirely. I keep going, fear driving me, until his neck is entirely gone and his head rolls away from his body.

Only then do I stop attacking, sure that he can no longer hurt me.

Only then do I look up to realize the courtyard is no longer empty.

My father's people and many of my half siblings stand around the edges. To a person, they stare at me with fear. I push slowly to my feet and several of them flinch away from me. I hate it. I never wanted to rule like this, but the men are right. Fear is the only way to ensure I survive this coup and keep surviving. There aren't any soldiers present, which is just as well. The men will take care of them. It's up to me to sell this once and for all.

I grab my father's head and hold it aloft. Someone cries out in horror. I ignore them and turn a slow circle, meeting as many gazes as I can manage, holding them until people look away. I lift his head and raise my voice. "I am my father's heir by virtue of the babe now growing in my womb. I am now the head of the clan by virtue of his death. Challenge me now or take a knee."

One of my brothers, William, steps forward. He opens his mouth but stops speaking as fire pours from my palm, turning our father's head to ash. I hold his gaze as I turn the fire on the body next. It burns hot, hot enough to flash dry the blood coating me, hot enough that the people closest take several large steps back. William shakes his head and sinks to one knee.

Fear truly is a powerful tool for a leader. The thought makes me vaguely ill, but there are no depths I won't descend to in order to protect the people I care about. I don't want to slaughter my way through my half siblings, but I'll do it if they force my hand.

William's taking the knee starts a waterfall effect, though. One by one, all the people around the courtyard kneel and bow their heads. I turn slowly, but not a single one of them will meet my gaze, let alone challenge me. *Thank the gods.* I refuse to let the relief show on my face.

Instead, I rotate to face William and lift my voice. "Gather everyone. It's time to make an announcement."

He doesn't look happy, but he nods. He turns to several people next to him. "Make the call."

It takes fifteen minutes for everyone in the compound to reach the courtyard. My hands still haven't returned to their normal shape and I'm still covered in my father's blood, but it's just as well. Again, not a single person challenges me as I declare myself the leader.

There will be challenges later, both martial and subtle, but it will take them at least a few days to gather their courage to try. A few days is all I need to cement my place here. I won't pretend that dueling will be easy, but after facing down my father, I'm not as worried as I was before. None of my half siblings' powers are as strong as his were. I can break their compulsions, which means I can win the fight.

There's another matter to attend to first, though. "Allow me to introduce you to my partners." I fling a hand over to where I feel Malachi, Rylan, and Wolf waiting. They leap over the bystanders and land at my back, a flashy move that almost makes me smile, especially when everyone gasps. Truly, my father's people are already conditioned to fall in line behind a strong leader. I have no intention of becoming a tyrant like my father, but I am not above taking advantage of the rotten foundation he left.

I will give them the strong leader they crave. Unlike my father, though, I won't abuse my power over them. I fully intend to be a queen they'll grow to love over time, or at least respect.

"You will obey these men as you would me." I wait for the murmured assent before continuing. "Now, go back to your homes and rest assured that you are safe. Your lives will not be negatively affected by this change in power." I hate that I find myself pitching my tone to mimic the way my father talked in public, that I'm using his cadences to ensure obedience from these people. I never set out to lead, but if I walk away and allow William or one of the others to take over, they will hunt me the same way our father did. I've made myself too much a threat to do anything but take my father's place. It's the only way.

"Do *not* force me to make an example of you." I sweep my gaze over them. "Go. Sleep. We will rebuild after everyone rests for the day."

The men fall behind me as I turn and head deeper into the compound. It's only when I take a familiar turn that I realize I'm walking back to my old room by habit and that it's not appropriate for me to sleep there if I'm supposed to be leading. It's just as well. That tiny room holds no good memories for me, and it's nowhere large enough for the four of us.

With a sigh, I veer in the opposite direction and make my way to my father's home. Stepping through the front door, even with my men at my back, feels like being launched into a past I want no part of. My knees buckle.

I never hit the floor.

Malachi scoops me up. "Bathroom?"

I try to speak, but no words come. Rylan brushes a hand over my head. "I'll get a shower going." He disappears through a doorway leading deeper into the house.

Wolf surveys the room. "I hope you're not attached to any of this." I shake my head mutely and he smiles. "Let Mal wind you down and we'll take care of the rest. You did good, love."

Malachi carries me through the house to the large bathroom Rylan found. Steam already curls through the air, and I take what feels like my first full breath in hours. We did it. We actually pulled it off. My father is gone and I am now the leader of this compound. *Holy shit.* I don't even know how to process that. I don't even know where to begin to start. "Oh gods." My body starts to shake, violent tremors hitting in waves. "It hurts." I don't know what I mean, only that it's true.

"I know, little dhampir. I know."

Rylan stays long enough to use his claws to divest me of my clothing and then he leaves, shutting the door softly behind him. Mal steps beneath the spray without setting me down. "Breathe. You did it. The worst of it is over."

"I never wanted to lead," I whisper. "I just wanted to be free."

"Freedom in our world comes at the price of power. This was the only way." He hugs me tightly. "Can you stand?"

"I think so?"

He sets me carefully on my feet and washes the blood from my body and hair. When he gets to my hands, he examines the claws. "These are impressive."

"I don't know how I did it. I just heard Rylan's voice in my head and then the magic obeyed."

"Sometimes it happens like that. Close your eyes." I obey, and he keeps speaking in that low, calm voice. "Envision your hands as they normally are. Not a claw or bit of fur in sight."

My eyes fly open. "I don't have *fur*."

He grins. "Now you don't have claws, either."

Sure enough, he's right. I wiggle the fingers of my very human hand. They look just like normal, feel just like normal. How strange. "That was easy."

"I did say it would get easier."

"I didn't think it would happen this fast." I take a deep breath and look at the door. "They're going to expect information and announcements and official things tomorrow."

"Yes. But you're not doing it alone." He presses his hand to my lower stomach. "You have us. I meant what I said last night. We will make this place the safest spot in the realms to raise our children. Anyone—*anyone*—who threatens us won't live long enough to regret it."

There was a time when I might say that's too bloodthirsty, but that time and that person are long gone. I nod. "Then I guess we best get started."

"Tomorrow, Mina."

When we leave the bathroom, clean and exhausted, it's to find that Rylan and Wolf have gutted the house. I look around with wide eyes. How did they possibly move this quickly? The living room is completely empty except for a plain mattress with what appears to be clean sheets sitting in the center of it. "What's this?"

Wolf saunters through the door. "Couldn't do the whole place in the time we had, but we figured you didn't want to be surrounded with memories of the monster." He eyes the mattress with distaste. "This is the largest we could find on short notice."

My lower lip quivers at the thoughtfulness of this. I *don't* want to be in this house, faced with the memory of my father, especially when it takes less than no effort to conjure how warm his blood was against my skin, how easily his flesh gave way to my claws. I shudder. "Thank you."

"Anything for you, love." He flops down onto the mattress.

Rylan steps into the house and shuts the door firmly behind himself. "I don't expect trouble tonight, but we'll keep an eye out for it." He frowns at Wolf. "Get off those clean sheets until you've had a shower."

"Right. Whoops." Wolf rolls easily to his feet and moves past me toward the shower. He brushes the backs of his fingers on my arm and then he's gone. A few seconds later, the shower starts up again.

Rylan comes to stand before me. "How are you doing?"

"I'm shaky and exhausted and overwhelmed." I try for a smile. "But we're all alive, so I'm good. Really good." I hesitate. "Lizzie?"

"Gone. I'm sure she'll be circling back at some point for that favor, but the Radu family will be doing what the rest of the clans are now that you've taken over." At my questioning look, he gives a wry smile. "Watching. Evaluating. Traditionally, there's a year grace period when someone ascends to head of clan, so we have that long to bolster our defenses and alliances and ensure we're too strong to reckon with."

"Oh," I say faintly. I've never heard of a grace period, but my father has ruled for a very, very long time. He was also tight-fisted with information as a way of controlling people—something I intend to change. I drag in a breath. "I guess we need to get started on that soon."

"Tomorrow," Malachi says firmly. "Everything can wait until tomorrow. Right now, we're going to hold you and we're going to celebrate the fact that we're alive and we won."

I find myself smiling slowly as he leads me to the bed. "I kind of like that plan."

"I thought you might." He smiles down at me, and for the first time since I met him, it's completely joyful and free of reserve. "I love you, little dhampir."

"I love you, too."

"Forever."

I go up onto my toes and kiss him. "*Forever.*"

19

FOUR YEARS LATER

I SMELL SMOKE AS I TURN DOWN THE HALL TOWARD the nursery. "Not again." I pick up my pace, sprinting the last few steps and throwing open the door, power at my fingertips and ready to quell the fire. The sight that greets me stops me short.

Rylan is sleeping in the rocking chair, the twins in his arms. They're still little, only three months, and they seem to have taken it as a personal challenge to see how ragged they can run the four of us. I'm more tired than I could have thought possible, but it's a good kind of tired. They're sleeping for once, so *they* aren't the source of the smoke.

No, the source is Wolf and Asher sitting on the floor across from each other, shooting little fireballs at each other. I start to yell a warning when Wolf sends one spiraling at our three-year-old, but he sends a little burst of power to fizzle it out well before it makes contact.

Then he turns and gives me an unrepentant grin. "He's even better at fire than you are."

"Mama!" Asher jumps to his feet and sprints to me, moving so quickly I barely get my arms out before he throws himself into them.

I spin him around twice and cuddle him close. "Hello, Trouble." I press a kiss to the top of his head, covered in dark curls. "Let's move this to the living room so the twins can sleep." I eye them. "Do you think it's wise to move them?"

"Rylan won't let them fall." Wolf hefts himself to his feet. "And you know what happened last time we tried to move them when they were sleeping."

I wince. Hours of sobbing and a particularly sleepless night. "We leave them then." Hopefully all three of them take a nice long nap. I turn and carry Asher out of the bedroom and down the hall to the living room. In the years since I took over the compound, everything's changed. Gone is my father's overbearing style, replaced by grounded, cozy furniture in pleasing colors. This house feels like a home for the first time in my life, and it's not solely because of the redecorating.

Malachi walks through the front door as we settle on the couch. He's dressed in a pair of jeans and a gray T-shirt and he's never looked better. He grins at the sight of us. "Someone said they smelled smoke, and I figured it was Asher getting up to no good."

"Wolf was supervising."

He glances at Wolf. "I bet he was."

We fully expected Asher to develop only one power, courtesy of whoever was his biological father, but in the last six months, he's shown evidence of all four bloodline powers that flow through his veins. We still don't know if it's courtesy of the bond I share with my men or because of some seraph quirk, but I'm already attempting to prepare myself for the chaos that will come when the twins start manifesting their powers. I hope we survive it.

Malachi crosses to press a kiss to my lips, then Wolf's, while he ruffles Asher's hair. "The twins?"

"They're taking a nap with Rylan."

His grin widens. "He does have the magic touch with them." It's true. They sleep better for Rylan than for any of us, though even that isn't saying much.

Next to me, Wolf clears his throat. "I heard from Lizzie."

I turn to look at him. "What? When?" She stopped by the compound exactly a year and a day after I took over the leadership, claiming it was to say congratulations for building a strong, stable community. In the three years since, she hasn't shown her face...or claimed the favor I owe her.

"Earlier."

I search his face for any evidence of distress and send a tentative probe along the bond. Wolf cracks his shields for me, allowing me in far enough to see that his calm isn't an act. I ease my magic away from him. "What did she want?"

"To call her favor due." He holds up a hand. "I'm fine. Things are different now than they were four years ago. We have people."

It's certainly true. While there was a small exodus of people in the weeks after I took over, the majority of the compound citizens stayed. In the time since, we've built up something special. The fear that originally held them in sway has given way to mutual respect and admiration. Wolf's right. We're stronger than we've ever been. Still, Lizzie presents a complication. "What favor?"

He gives a mirthless smile. "She wants us to entertain the Radu clan for a week."

"No. Absolutely not."

"Yes." He covers my hand with his. "You already have her word that they won't cause harm to any of ours. We'll get it from my mother as well. It will be fine."

I narrow my eyes. "You're taking this rather calmly." Far more calmly than he did when Rylan's mother came to visit. I shudder a little at the memory. She didn't do anything out of line, but I've never met a scarier person in my life. I'm not eager to repeat the experience with Wolf's mother. "I thought you'd want to avoid it."

"I thought she'd be here within the second year. The fact that we've had this long is a boon." He shrugs. "Like I said, we have people."

I twist to catch Malachi's eye. "How do you feel about this?"

"He's right. We're too strong to fuck with."

"Fuck with," Asher says.

I shoot Malachi a murderous look. "No, baby, those are grown-up words and only grown-ups are allowed to use them."

"Fuck, fuck, fuck." Asher wiggles out of my arms and practically bounces from one piece of furniture to another. "Fuck!" He sends a tiny fireball shooting at a painting I bought during one of our trips last year.

Malachi snuffs it out quickly. "That's enough of that." He gives me one last kiss and scoops up Asher. "It's bath time. No more fireballs, no more bad language."

Asher gives him a look like he might test this new boundary but ultimately decides bath time is more important. He smiles like a perfect little child who wasn't just shouting expletives and shooting fireballs. "Yes, Daddy."

"Thought so." He stops in the doorway. "We have time to figure out the Radu stuff, but don't worry, little dhampir. There's nothing to fear."

I take a slow breath and let it out as he disappears down the hall. He's right. I take Wolf's hand and squeeze it. "You're really okay with this?"

"More or less." He shrugs. "It was bound to happen at some point. No matter how crazy my family is, they value children. They just want to poke their nose into our business and test our defenses a little. Nothing will come of it." He makes a face. "The same can't be true when the children are adults, but that's a bridge we'll cross when we get there."

"Hey, I love you." I wait for him to look back at me. "If they come here and cross the line, then we'll kill them and you never have to deal with them again."

Wolf lets out that glorious laugh that I love so much. "There's my murderous woman." He pulls me into his lap. "I love you, too. We'll get through the visit without murder." He grins, bright and sharp. "But I appreciate the sentiment all the same."

I never thought to end up happy in this compound. I certainly never thought I'd have built a life with three men. But...I've never been happier. The thought of living a life that stretches for hundreds of years used to scare me, but each day now brings something new and wonderful. Even the bad stuff isn't world-ending because I'm not facing it alone.

I'll never have to face it alone ever again.

And neither will my men.

EPILOGUE

THE DEMON REALM

EVERYTHING WAS IN ITS PLACE.

Azazel surveyed the room one last time. The low stage stood at the front of it, just wide enough to fit five humans standing side by side. The room was arranged carefully, seating grouped just far enough away from each other that it made a confrontation less likely, all arranged in a half circle equal distances from the stage. Politics bored him, but they were necessary to navigate from time to time.

Like now.

After tonight, he would have what he wanted most. In addition to that, all four leaders of the other territories in this realm would owe him a favor. The women had been prepped and the contracts were good on their end. All that was left was to auction them off, get the second set of contracts signed and those bargains cemented.

Then he could focus on his reward.

Thane was the first to arrive, and he came alone. He nodded to Azazel and sank into the low pool built into the floor. The dark water hid the tentacles taking up the lower half of his body and nearly matched his dark gray skin.

Next came Bram, his wings tucked tight against his body. He eyed Thane and made a wide, pointed circle around his pool. Air and water rarely got along, but this was ridiculous. He finally sank into the backless chair ready for him. "This better be worth the trip, Azazel."

"Oh, it will be."

Thunderous footsteps signaled Sol's arrival. Azazel knew for a fact the dragon could tread silently when he chose, but why bother with that when he could shake the building instead. He stalked through the door, glanced around, and made a beeline for the stool with a divot in the back to accommodate his thick tail.

Rusalka, of course, was last. She always liked to make an entrance. She came through the door with her hair floating in an uncanny current. Flames burned beneath her flesh, so bright in places, it almost hurt to look at her. She was nearly as tall as Sol and had the most human body of all of them...as long as one ignored the fiery skin that would burn anyone who touched her without permission. He'd seen it happen before, and she'd laughed while the poor bastard died at her feet.

"Thank you for coming. I think you'll find tonight's offerings to your taste." As if any of them had tastes for *this* kind of offering. Humans in their realm were few and far between; he had brought most of them over years ago. They—and their

bloodlines—were a rare enough commodity to get all these leaders in the same room for the first time in generations. "The price
will be the same regardless."

"I'm sure." Rusalka draped one leg over the other, her cloven
hoof tapping the ground. "We're not giving our lands up for a
piece of ass, Azazel. Be serious."

"I don't want your lands." Being the ultimate leader of this
realm would be more trouble than it was worth. "I want peace.
The constant warring is draining our resources faster than we can
replenish them. You all know that or you wouldn't be here. It's
time for a new generation of leaders to do things our way." He
motioned to the doorway on one side of the stage. "The peace
offering."

One by one, five women filed out onto the stage.

Azazel turned to the gathered leaders. "Now, we make our
selections."

KEEP READING FOR A LOOK AT *WICKED BEAUTY* BY KATEE ROBERT

1

HELEN

"I AM SO FUCKING LATE," I MUTTER UNDER MY BREATH. The hallways of Dodona Tower are blessedly empty, but that only makes the clock ticking down inside my head worse. Tonight is the night everything changes. The night when I stop being a pawn in other people's games and finally gain the agency I've craved ever since I was a little girl.

And I can't believe I'm fucking *late*.

I pick up my pace, barely managing to resist the urge to run. Showing up out of breath and flustered to an Olympus party is even worse than showing up late. Appearances matter. It's been a long time since Olympus experienced anything resembling traditional warfare, but every day, little battles are fought and won using the most mundane things.

A carefully designed dress.

A sweet word hiding a poisonous sting.

A marriage.

I duck into the elevator that will take me up to the ballroom floor and barely resist the urge to bounce on my toes with impatience. Normally, I wouldn't give a damn about any of this. I make petty rebellions an art form.

Tonight is different.

Tonight, my brother Perseus—Zeus, now—is making an announcement that will change everything.

Less than a week ago, Ares passed away. It was hardly unexpected—the man was old as dirt and had been knocking on the doors to the underworld for three months—but it's opened up an opportunity that's usually only seen once a generation. Of the Thirteen, Ares alone is open to absolutely anyone. A person's history, connections, finances don't matter. You don't even have to be Olympian.

You simply have to win.

Three trials, all designed to cull the wheat from the chaff, and the last person standing steps up to become Ares. One of the thirteen people who create the ruling body in Olympus. Each handles a specific part of keeping the city running smoothly, but more importantly to me, no one can compel any of them to take an action they don't want to.

Not even Zeus can force the hand of another member of the Thirteen—or at least that's the theory. My father never paid attention to those sorts of niceties, and I doubt my brother will now that he's inherited the title. It doesn't matter. If I'm Ares, I'm no longer daughter to one Zeus, sister to another, a spoiled princess with no real value beyond her pretty face and family connections.

Becoming Ares will set me free.

The elevator doors open, and I hurry in the direction of the ballroom. The long hallway has changed since the last party, the dour, dark drapes that hung floor to ceiling on either side of the doors replaced with an airy white fabric that has silver threaded through it. It's still not welcoming, but it's significantly less oppressive.

I'm curious who made *that* design call, because Perseus sure as fuck didn't. Since he stepped up as Zeus after our father's death, the only thing my oldest brother cares about is running his business and ruling Olympus with an iron fist.

Or at least trying to.

"Helen."

I stop short, but recognition brings a relieved smile to my face. "Eros. What are you doing out here lurking in the shadows?"

He steps forward and holds up a tiny jeweled bag. "Psyche forgot her purse." He should look ridiculous holding the purse, especially considering the violence those hands have done, but Eros has a habit of moving through life as if he's untouchable. No one would dare say a word and he knows it.

"What a good husband you are." I take the last few steps and press a quick kiss to each of his cheeks. I haven't seen him much in the last couple months, but he looks good. Eros is one of the most gorgeous people in Olympus—which is saying something—a white guy with curly blond hair and a face to make painters weep at its perfection. "Marriage suits you."

"More and more every day." His gaze sharpens. "You've pulled out all the stops tonight."

"Do you like the dress?" I smooth my hands down my gown. It's a custom piece, the golden fabric molded to my body from shoulders to hips before flaring out the slightest bit. It's heavy with a subtle pattern that's designed to catch the light with every move. A deep V dips between my breasts, and the shoulders have been shaped into sharp points that give the slightest impression of military bearing. "It's a showstopper, as my mother would have said."

I ignore the twinge in my chest at the thought, just as I always do when my mind tries to linger on the woman who died far too young. She's been gone fifteen years, having suffered a *mysterious* fall when I was fifteen. Mysterious. Right. As if all of Olympus didn't suspect that my father was behind it.

As if I didn't know it for certain.

Pushing *this* thought away is second nature. It doesn't matter what sins my father committed. He's dead and gone, just like my mother. I hope he's been suffering in the pits of Tartarus since he drew his last breath. When I think of his death, all I feel is relief. He died before he could marry me off to secure some bullshit alliance, before he could cause even more of the pain he seemed to enjoy inflicting so much.

No, I don't miss my father at all.

"She'd be proud of you."

"Maybe." I glance over his shoulder at the doors. "Maybe she'd be furious over what I'm about to do." Rock the boat? Fuck, I'm about to tip the boat right over.

Eros doesn't miss a beat. His brows rise and he shakes his

head, looking rueful. "So it's Ares for you. I should have known. You've been missing a lot of parties lately. Training?"

"Yes." I brace myself for his disbelief. We might be friends, but we're friends by Olympus standards. I trust Eros not to slide a knife between my ribs. He trusts me not to cause him undue trouble in the press. We hang out on a regular basis at events and parties and occasionally trade favors. I don't trust him with my deepest secrets. It's nothing personal. I don't trust *anyone* with that part of me.

On the other hand, everyone in Olympus will know my plans very shortly.

I square my shoulders. "I'm going to compete to become the next Ares."

"Damn." He whistles under his breath. "You've got your work cut out for you."

He's not telling me he thinks he can't do it, but I wilt a little all the same. I didn't *really* expect enthusiastic support, but being constantly underestimated never fails to sting. "Yes, well, I'd better get in there."

"Hold on." He surveys me. "Your hair is a little lopsided."

"*What?*" I lift my hand and touch my head. I can't tell without a mirror. Damn it, I'm going to be even later, but it's still better than walking into that room out of sorts.

I start to turn in the direction of the bathroom back toward the elevators, but Eros catches my shoulder. "I got it." He opens Psyche's purse and digs around for a few seconds, pulling out an even smaller bag. Inside, there is a bunch of bobby pins. Eros huffs out a laugh at my incredulous expression. "Don't look so surprised. If you had a purse, you'd have bobby pins stashed, too. Now, hold still and let me fix your shit."

Shock roots me in place as he carefully fixes my hair, securing it with half a dozen bobby pins. He leans back and nods. "Better."

"Eros." I gently touch my hair again. "Since when do you do hair?"

He shrugs. "I can't do more than damage control, but it saves Psyche some trouble when we're out if I can help like this."

Gods, he's so in love it makes me sick. I'm happy for him. Truly, I am. But I can't help the jealousy that curls through me. It's not about Eros—he's more brother to me than anything else— but at the intimacy and trust he shares with his wife. The one time I thought I might have that, it blew up in my face, and I still wear the emotional scars from the fallout.

I manage a smile, though. "Thanks."

"Knock 'em dead, Helen." His grin is sharp enough to cut. "I'll be rooting for you."

I drag in a slow breath and turn for the door. Since I'm late, I might as well make an entrance. I straighten my spine and push both doors open with more force than necessary. People scatter as I step into the room. I pause, letting them look at me and taking them in at the same time.

This room has changed since Perseus inherited the title of Zeus. Oh, the space is still functionally the same. Shining white marble floors that I can barely see beneath the crowd, an arching ceiling that gives the impression of the ballroom being even larger than it is, the massive windows and glass doors that lead out to the balcony on the other side of the room. But it still feels different. The walls used to be cream, but now they're a cool gray. A subtle change, but it makes a difference.

Most notably, the larger-than-life portraits of the Thirteen that line the walls have different frames. Gone are the thick gold frames that my father favored, replaced by finely crafted black. I would have to get closer to verify, but each looks like they might be custom, unique to each member of the Thirteen.

Perseus didn't make these changes, either. I'm certain of it. Our father might have been obsessive about his image, but my brother doesn't give a fuck. Even when he should.

I start through the crowd, holding my head high.

Normally, I can identify every single person who attends a Dodona Tower party. Information is everything, and I learned from a very young age that it's the only weapon I'm allowed. Some people meet my gaze, others stare at my body in a way that makes my skin crawl, and still others all but turn their backs on me. No surprises there. Being a Kasios in Olympus might have its perks, but it means being born into generations-old grudges and politicking. I grew up learning who could be trusted—no one—and who would actually shove me into traffic if given half a chance—more people than is comforting.

But this party isn't a regular one, and tonight is not a regular night. Nearly half the faces are new to me, people who have arrived from the outskirts around Olympus or been ferried into the city by Poseidon for this special occasion. I don't stop moving to memorize faces. Not everyone here will be nominating themselves as champions; plenty of them are just like the majority of the people here from Olympus. Hangers-on. They don't matter.

I don't pick up my pace, moving at a steady stalk that forces people to get out of my way. The crowd parts for me just like I know it will, whispers following in my wake. I'm making a scene, and while half of them love me for it, the rest resent me.

Everyone has pulled out all the stops tonight. In one corner, my sister Eris—Aphrodite, as of three months ago—is laughing at something with Hermes and Dionysus. My chest gives a pang. I would like nothing more than to be with them now, just like I am at every other party. My sister and my friends are what makes living in Olympus bearable, but the last few months have driven home the new differences between us. It wasn't so noticeable when Eris was still Eris, but now that she's also one of the Thirteen...

I'm getting left behind. Being sister to Zeus and Aphrodite, friend to Hermes and Dionysus? It doesn't mean shit. I'm still a piece to be moved around on someone else's board.

Becoming Ares is my only opportunity to change that.

ABOUT THE AUTHOR

Katee Robert is a *New York Times* and *USA Today* bestselling author of contemporary romance and romantic suspense. *Entertainment Weekly* calls her writing "unspeakably hot." Her books have sold over a million copies. She lives in the Pacific Northwest with her husband, children, a cat who thinks he's a dog, and two Great Danes who think they're lap dogs. You can visit her at kateerobert.com or on Twitter @katee_robert.